PELICANS, PIERS AND POISON

DUNE HOUSE COZY MYSTERY SERIES

CINDY BELL

CONTENTS

Copyright © 2019 Cindy Bell

All rights reserved.

Cover Design by Annie Moril

All rights reserved. No part of this publication may be reproduced or transmitted in any form or by any means, electronic or mechanical, including photocopy, recording, or any information storage or retrieval system, without permission in writing from the publisher.

This is a work of fiction. The characters, incidents and locations portrayed in this book and the names herein are fictitious. Any similarity to or identification with the locations, names, characters or history of any person, product or entity is entirely coincidental and unintentional.

All trademarks and brands referred to in this book are for illustrative purposes only, are the property of their respective owners and not affiliated with this publication in any way. Any trademarks are being used without permission, and the publication of the trademark is not authorized by, associated with or sponsored by the trademark owner.

ISBN: 9781093423242

ary Brent adjusted the flowers in a large vase in the center of the dining room table. As her fingertips glided over the thin, green stems, she smiled to herself. She enjoyed everything about them, from their delicate scent, to their silky petals. It had nothing to do with the fact that she'd received them as a gift from a certain detective. She reorganized the flowers one more time then took a step back. Everything in the dining room appeared inviting and warm. She'd been working with her friend, Suzie Allen, to create a more homey look in the dining room and living room of Dune House, their majestic bed and breakfast on the beach. She'd found that most of their guests appreciated a cozy vibe when they first walked in the door. Although interior design wasn't her specialty, she'd picked up a few tips from living and working with Suzie for so long.

"Oh, those look fantastic." Suzie smiled as she stepped in through the front door. "Where did you get them? I didn't think you went anywhere this morning."

"I didn't." Mary's cheeks flushed as she glanced away from the flowers. "Someone dropped them off."

"Oh, I see." Suzie's smile spread into a grin. "That Wes has turned into quite the charmer, hasn't he?"

"I think so." Mary laughed. "How are things looking on the beach?"

"Well, it's not warm enough for swimming, but I did put some chairs and tables down by the water in case our guests want to enjoy the view up close." Suzie stretched her arms out above her head. "It was good to get out there in the sunlight. I've been stuck in that room upstairs trying to get things just right, and I forgot about how much I need some nature in my life."

"How is it going in there?" Mary pulled out a chair at the table and sat down.

"It's getting there. I think a few more accent

pieces and we'll have a redecorated guest room to offer, it will be like it's brand new. I'd love to do some antiquing this weekend. Do you think we could squeeze it in?" Suzie pulled out a chair beside Mary and sat down as well.

"I don't see why not. We only have one couple coming into town, and I'm sure they will have their own plans that will fill their time while they are here." Mary tipped her head to the side. "I heard there is a new antique store opening in Parish. It might be a good time to check it out."

"Oh, that sounds perfect." Suzie clapped her hands in the same moment that someone knocked on the front door.

"Who is that?" Mary stood up from her chair. "I didn't think anyone was due to come by?"

"Not sure. I'll have a look." Suzie stood up as well, just as the front door began to swing open.

"Hello? Anyone here?" A young woman poked her head into the bed and breakfast.

"Hi there." Suzie smiled as she looked at her. A quick assessment told her that she didn't know the woman, which if she was a local, was unusual in the small town of Garber. "Come on in."

"Thanks." She smiled as she stepped farther inside. Another young woman walked in behind her.

"I'm sorry to intrude, could I have just a few minutes of your time?"

"What are you selling?" Suzie raised an eyebrow.

"Not exactly selling anything." She stepped all the way into the foyer, as Suzie and Mary stood up to greet her. She held a few pamphlets in her hand. "My name is Hannah and this is one of my waitresses, Justine. I'm just making an effort to reach out to the local businesses that might be interested in what our new restaurant has to offer." She smiled as she met them just beside the living room. "It's called Pelicans on the Pier. Have you heard of it? I own it."

"Yes, actually." Mary met her eyes. "It's surprising to have a new restaurant in town. What brought you to Garber?"

"I visited the area a few years ago with my family, and I just loved the setting. It's such a quaint little town, and the people are all so close-knit. I thought it would be the perfect place to introduce my vision of a restaurant. When the building at the end of the pier came up for sale, I knew it was the perfect time." Hannah held out the pamphlets. "I brought you some menus in case you'd like to share them with your guests as an option for dining."

"Thanks." Suzie took the pamphlets and glanced at the cover. It featured a long picnic style dining table with several main dishes in the center of it. "We usually recommend the diner or Cheney's Restaurant, though."

"I understand. I'm sure Cheney's is a fine establishment." Hannah clasped her hands together in front of her. "But we offer something a little different. Ever since I became a waitress, I noticed that restaurants all tend to have one theme. The people that come to dine at them are isolated from each other. They're at separate tables or facing away from each other. No one is encouraged to interact. Some of my fondest memories are of my entire family getting together over a large meal, chatting and interacting as we passed the dishes around. That is the kind of dining I think we need more of right now. My restaurant offers a place for people to not only share a meal, but share conversation, and get to know their neighbors."

"So, everyone is seated together?" Mary raised an eyebrow. "How does the ordering process work?"

"We feature a different menu every night. We always include a selection of seafood. We also offer individual sides that can be selected. So, if you'd like roast potatoes to be on the table, they will be, but we make enough for everyone to share." Hannah shrugged and smiled. "That way not only are you getting something you enjoy, but you can introduce your favorite foods to others."

"What about payment?" Suzie tipped her head to the side. "How does that work?"

"The price is the same for everyone. It is twenty dollars to dine, and that includes a drink. You can order additional drinks such as wine or beer for a fee that you pay at the time of serving." Hannah tapped the menu in Suzie's hand. "All of the details are inside. It takes the pressure off deciding what to order, you get a truly home-cooked meal with all of the sides that you love, and you get to share quality time with an entire table full of your friends and neighbors and possibly even some strangers, instead of only one or two people that you already probably know fairly well. It gives you the opportunity to meet new people and it brings a lot of excitement to the conversations. People are welcome to serve themselves as much as they would like until the food runs out. Not much gets wasted, and everyone is satisfied in the end."

"That's really an interesting concept." Mary smiled. "It reminds me of the family dinners my children and I would share. We always managed to talk about everything under the sun during dinner."

"I hope you'll come in to try it out. I'm sure you'd like it." Hannah smiled.

"I'm sure we will." Mary nodded. "Good luck with your new business."

"Thank you." Hannah nodded to Suzie, then turned and left the house. Justine followed after her.

"Okay, out with it." Mary glanced over at Suzie.

"Out with what?" Suzie carried the menus over to the small desk set up between the dining room and the foyer where she and Mary checked guests in. She set the menus on the top of the desk, then turned back to look at Mary.

"You didn't say a word. I know what that means. You're too polite to say what you're thinking sometimes." Mary grinned.

"I just don't see how that could be very enjoyable. I mean, everyone squashed together and sharing food?" Suzie scrunched up her nose. "I know we sit down to meals with our guests, but that is more intimate, there aren't so many people, there is lots of room and we don't share all the food in the middle of the table. I guess I'm a little too much of an introvert for that."

"You can't know if you like it until you try it." Mary gave her a light pat on the shoulder. "It really can get interesting when you have a lot of different personalities at the same table with you. You enjoy chatting with our guests."

"Hmm, I guess it's worth a shot sometime. Although, I hate to think of the competition it gives Cheney's. This town is too small to have two sit-down family restaurants. And I heard that Cheney's wanted to move to that building on the pier because of the view and pelicans around there, but they were outbid." Suzie looked back at the front door. "I admire anyone who wants to give a new idea a try, but I don't think Garber is the right place for it."

"I guess we'll find out either way, soon enough." Mary shrugged. "I'm going to take Pilot for a walk before the guests are due to arrive, that way he will be too worn out to cause too much trouble."

"Good luck." Suzie laughed as she thought of their ever-energetic pup.

CHAPTER 2

A flutter of the curtains in the front window drew Suzie's attention. The porcelain flower she'd just dusted clinked against the glass of the side table as she set it down. Through the window, shadows of seagulls swirled across the parking lot. She glanced at the clock on the wall and watched the second hand tick in a slow circle.

"Any minute now." Suzie smiled to herself, then quickly stepped into the kitchen. She popped open the cabinet under the sink and stowed the dust cloth inside. As she passed the toaster, she paused and tucked a few wayward hairs back behind her ears. After a deep breath, she surveyed the kitchen and dining room on the way back towards the front door. Although the bed and breakfast had been doing well, this time of the year always proved to be a little slow, and she knew that every review counted. Something as simple as cobwebs in a corner, or a pile of unfolded laundry could impact the words she read splashed all over the internet. She hoped that this couple would leave a glowing review and recommend Dune House to all of their friends.

"What are their names again?" Mary squeezed a throw pillow, then gave it a light punch before dropping it into just the right place on the couch.

"Sam and Ginger." Suzie's eyes flicked towards the window again. "Ginger sounded very sweet on the phone when she made the reservations."

"Great. It would be nice if they're a little low maintenance."

"We shall see." Suzie laughed, then took a sharp breath as she noticed a car pull into the parking lot. "It looks like they're here. Let me gather up the paperwork. Will you greet them?"

"Sure." Mary smoothed down the front of her simple, denim dress, then walked towards the front door. She swung it open just as Sam's knuckles made contact with the door. In his late twenties, Sam looked a little older than that, with a few strands of gray in his hair and wrinkles around his eyes that deepened as he smiled.

"Good timing."

"We're eager to have you." Mary grinned as she looked past him towards the woman who stood just behind him. Ginger's petite frame seemed even smaller beside her husband's rotund physique. The only thing big about her was the mop of dark curls that billowed around her face. Although Mary knew she was about the same age as her husband, she looked quite a bit younger. "Welcome to Dune House." She smiled as she gestured for them to step inside. "Please, come in."

"Wow, the pictures on the website don't do this place justice." Ginger placed her hands on her hips as she looked over the foyer that led into the dining room. "It's homey, but it's also huge."

"Does it get drafty at night?" Sam scrunched up his nose as he lugged their bags inside. "I mean, places like this are so hard to heat, aren't they?"

"Actually, it's pretty well insulated." Mary led them towards the living room. "We did a lot of renovations, but it was also well constructed to begin with. But if you do find it chilly, there are plenty of extra blankets, and we can always adjust the thermostat. We also have a fireplace." She paused just inside the living room door and tipped her head towards the fireplace that took up a good portion of one wall.

"Isn't that nice?" Ginger smiled. "So much better than a boring, old hotel."

"Maybe." Sam grunted.

Mary assessed the couple as she sensed some tension between them. Ginger wore a brightly colored dress that flowed around her slender body. Sam wore nothing but gray from top to bottom, even his shoes were gray and carefully tied into perfectly balanced bows. His style screamed order and precision. She guessed that it was Ginger's suggestion to book the bed and breakfast instead of a hotel.

"Your room is all prepared for you, if you'd like to get settled." Mary glanced over at Suzie as she entered the living room. "I'm Mary, and this is Suzie. You can pick up any line in the house and it will connect to our cell phones, in case there is anything you need."

"I just have a tiny bit of paperwork for you to fill out." Suzie handed them a clipboard with a few papers stacked on it. "It's a bit chilly for swimming, but the beach is beautiful. I'd highly recommend spending some time on it."

"We plan to." Ginger grinned. "Don't we, Sam?"

"Yes, definitely." Sam pulled the pen out of the clipboard and began to scrawl across the paperwork.

"I hope you both enjoy your time here." Suzie smiled as she handed Ginger a few pamphlets. "There are several places that you might like to visit or explore while you're here. We do offer breakfast and dinner, but if you'd rather dine at a local establishment, I'd recommend Cheney's. Their food and service are both wonderful."

"This looks interesting." Ginger pulled out one of the pamphlets. "Pelicans on the Pier?"

"Oh yes, that's a new restaurant in town." Suzie shrugged. "I haven't eaten there yet, so I can't personally recommend it, but if you try it, please let me know what you think."

"We will." Ginger smiled as she tucked the pamphlet into her purse.

"Here you go." Sam handed the clipboard back to Suzie. "When we travel, we like to experience the local restaurants, so we will be eating out for all our meals."

"I understand." Suzie nodded. "But you are always welcome. Just let us know if you change your mind. If you're ever hungry for a snack the kitchen is well-stocked, and you are welcome to forage through it."

"Sure." Sam reached for their suitcases. "I'll take these to our room."

"Sam, no." Ginger laughed and pulled him away from the suitcases. "First things first, we're going to the beach."

"Ginger, we should get unpacked and settled first." Sam sighed as he gazed at her.

"Nonsense. I am going to loosen you up on this trip if it kills me, or you." Ginger laughed and grabbed his hand, then tugged him towards the sliding glass doors in the dining room. "We'll have plenty of time to get settled once the sun goes down."

"But then we'll be too tired and—" Sam huffed as Ginger shot him a sharp look. "Fine, yes, whatever you want."

"Enjoy." Suzie waved to them as they stepped out through the sliding doors in the dining room, onto the wide porch. She watched as they descended the steps onto the path that led to the beach. It always gave her a subtle jolt of happiness to see how dazzled guests were by the beauty of Garber. She understood the feeling well as she had felt it herself when she first arrived in the seaside town. For having such beautiful views, it had managed to remain a relatively quiet place, and the combination of that and the wonderful people that lived there, made it Suzie's favorite place to be.

"Well, I guess we don't have to worry about meals." Mary smiled as she watched them go. "That certainly frees a lot of our time up. I'll make sure they have some breakfast options and coffee in the morning just in case."

"Sounds good." Suzie stared after them. "That Sam is a little grumpy, hopefully the beach will loosen him up a bit."

"I hope so, too." Mary jumped as her cell phone rang. "I'll never get used to having that thing go off in my pocket." She laughed as she fished it out of a large pocket on her dress. "Oh, it's Wes, do you mind if I take this?"

"Of course not. Enjoy." Suzie smiled and walked off towards the kitchen. As she began to wash off the few dishes in the sink she thought about Paul, out on the water. His boat was due to come in that evening. She wasn't sure if they'd be able to meet for dinner when she last spoke to him, but now she knew she would be free. She looked forward to spending some time with him. As a fisherman, he was often out on the water for days or weeks at a time. Although she didn't mind the time apart, she did very much enjoy the homecomings. Paul always smelled of salt, and sun, and he wrapped his arms around her so tight that she imagined he worried she might just float away. She never thought she'd be caught up in a romance in her fifties, and yet just the thought of Paul sent her heart racing. As if he sensed her thoughts, her phone began to ring. She dried off her hands and answered the call.

"You must be close if you have enough service to call me." Suzie smiled.

"Not close enough." Paul sighed. "I might be delayed a bit this evening."

"Oh no, bad weather?"

"Not exactly. I'm having some trouble with the boat, and the winds aren't helping."

"Is everything okay?" Suzie's heart skipped a beat. "Maybe you should have the coastguard come out and help you."

"I'll be fine." Paul chuckled. "You act like you worry about me or something."

"Me?" Suzie smiled. "You know better than that."

"I can't wait to see you. But if you're busy with your guests I understand."

"I won't be. I'll be there, when you get home."

Suzie's cheeks warmed at the comment. Was she being too clingy? Did he imagine her standing on the dock, desperately seeking some sign of his boat? "I mean, if you'd like me to be."

"I can't think of anything I'd like better. See you soon, Suzie." Paul ended the call.

Suzie shook her head, tucked her phone back into the pocket of her jeans, and continued with the dishes. If she wasn't careful, she'd definitely ruin her reputation of being independent and casual.

CHAPTER 3

*L*ater that evening, after ensuring that there were extra towels and blankets in the linen closet adjacent to the guests' room, Suzie changed out of her jeans into a nicer pair of pants and a pale blue blouse. She liked to dress up a bit when she went to Cheney's, and she liked dressing up for Paul. She brushed her fingers back through her shoulder length hair and glanced briefly in the mirror. Satisfied, she headed to the living room.

"Oh, don't you look beautiful." Mary smiled as she turned to look at her.

"Me?" Suzie grinned as she swept her gaze over the dress Mary wore. "That's a far cry from denim."

"It is, isn't it?" Mary ran her hand along the gauzy material of her skirt. "I thought since we're trying out the new place, I'd put on something a bit more respectable. Though, to be honest, I'm not sure what that is."

"You look fantastic." Suzie gave her a quick hug.

"You're sure you don't want to try out the new place with us?" Mary brushed a few strands of auburn hair behind her ear. "It might be fun for the four of us to do it together."

"We have family style dinner here at least once a week." Suzie smiled. "Sorry, I'd rather go to Cheney's, I'm dying for some of those delicious garlic knots they serve there."

"Oh yes, those are good." Mary inched closer to her. "Maybe you could bring some home for me."

"Of course, I will." Suzie laughed. "As long as you give me the scoop on the food at Pelicans on the Pier. I might be willing to try it out if there is something really tasty there."

"I'll make sure I give you a full review." Mary glanced at her watch. "Isn't Paul supposed to be getting in soon?"

"Yes, but he ran into some issues with the boat. I'm going to head down to the dock in a little while to meet him. I'll make sure Pilot has his food first." Suzie checked her phone. "And I'll be on call in case there is any issue with the guests. Please, go enjoy your evening with Wes, I know with his busy schedule it's hard for the two of you to get a night out together."

"Thanks Suzie." Mary smoothed down the front of her dress and cringed. "I feel a little silly in this."

"You don't look silly." Suzie walked with her to the door. "Is Wes picking you up?"

"Yes, he'll be here any minute." Mary poked her head out through the door. "Oh actually, I think he just pulled up."

"Have fun."

"You too." Mary waved to her over her shoulder.

Suzie waved to Wes as he got out of the car to open Mary's door.

Wes smiled as he tipped his hat in her direction. There were some benefits to having a police detective from the neighboring town in their circle of friends. Not quite as many benefits as having a cousin for a detective in the same town, but still a wonderful addition to their strange crew.

As Suzie went to check on Pilot's food, the eager Yellow Labrador came up to greet her. As she crouched down and ruffled her fingers through his warm, soft fur, she felt her muscles relax. Pilot had been a surprise addition to their household, but now she couldn't imagine her life without him.

After Suzie settled Pilot and checked his food, she decided to walk down to the dock. She guessed that Paul would arrive soon, and she didn't mind spending some time looking at the water. When she reached the dock, she noticed that there were quite a few boats in. Perhaps the weather was preparing to turn. She leaned against the railing and looked out over the water. She could recall the first few times she'd waited for Paul to arrive. Of course, she had pretended that she wasn't waiting, but she was. She smiled to herself as she thought about those first nervous moments when she wondered if she could even be in a relationship with him. Now, she wondered how she had ever doubted their connection. As time slipped by, the air grew cooler. She hadn't exactly dressed for being out in the elements as the sun set. She had assumed that Paul would be back before it got completely dark. She began to walk along the dock to keep herself warm.

"Hey there, gorgeous, care to take a walk with me?" A voice called out to her. Paul jogged along the dock towards her. He reached for her hand, just as she pulled it away.

"No, sorry, I'm waiting for someone." Suzie raised an eyebrow as she turned away from him.

"Any man that would leave you waiting is a fool." Paul slid his hand along her lower back in an attempt to wrap his arm around her.

"Oh, he's no fool." Suzie crossed her arms. "He's just a very hard worker and dedicated to his career."

"Is that so?" Paul leaned closer to her, his voice soft. "I still say he's a fool."

"You're wrong." Suzie turned to face him and looked into his eyes. "But it would be pretty foolish of him to play games with me when I'm starving."

"Okay, okay." Paul grinned and caught her hand in his. "Let's go eat." He brought her hand to his lips and placed a light kiss on the back of it.

"Wonderful." Suzie smiled as she held his gaze. "Where is your boat? I didn't see you pull in."

"I had to come in at the far dock, too crowded here tonight, and I need the extra room to do some repairs." Paul sighed. "I hope you're not upset that I'm late?" He slid his arm around her as they walked towards the restaurant.

"Of course not, I know things come up." Suzie wrapped her arm around his waist. "I'm just glad you're here now. I can't wait to get my hands on some of those garlic knots."

"Me either." He grinned.

Soft lighting illuminated the sidewalk outside of Cheney's. The outside tables lined the length of the restaurant.

"On an evening with nice weather like this, I'm surprised that there's no one sitting outside." Suzie peeked inside as Paul opened the door for her. "Oh, wow Paul. There's hardly anyone here."

"Good for us." Paul grinned as he steered her towards their favorite table. "We should get fast service."

"Great, because just in case I didn't mention it earlier, I'm starving." Suzie grinned as she settled at the table.

"Are you?" Paul raised an eyebrow. "I had no idea. Hmm." He rubbed his hand along his chin. "It might take me awhile to decide on what I want."

"Stop teasing me." Suzie laughed and flagged down a waiter.

By the time their food arrived, a few more people had arrived at the restaurant.

"I bet this poor turnout is because of that new restaurant." Suzie took a sip of her wine. "Mary went there tonight with Wes."

"Traitors." Paul winked at her.

"I told her to let me know if they have any good

food." Suzie smiled as she saw their tray of food arriving. "Oh yes, bring me those garlic knots."

"I hope you both enjoy." The waiter set their plates down on the table.

"Thanks so much." Suzie's eyes widened at the sight of the food. A feast at Cheney's was one of her favorite ways to splurge.

"I know exactly who you are!" A shout suddenly carried through the mostly quiet restaurant as a man lunged out of his chair towards another man. He stood to his full height, which Suzie guessed had to be well over six feet. She estimated him to be in his late thirties or early forties. She recognized him as a local businessman named Travis, but not the man he shouted at.

"I don't know what you're talking about." The other much shorter man, who appeared to be in his thirties, stood up from his chair as well. "Just calm down."

"Calm down?" Travis stormed away from his table towards the younger man. The woman that was seated with Travis stared at him with wide eyes. "Don't pretend you don't know who I am. You stalked me. You took pictures of me. You ruined my life."

"Back off." The other man raised his hands in

the air. "If you take a step closer to me, I will call the police."

"Too late for that," Suzie muttered to Paul as she tipped her head towards the waiter who had just hung up the phone near the register.

"I should break this up." Paul started to stand up, but Suzie put her hand on his arm.

"Just let it play out. No one is hurting anyone. You getting in the middle might only make things more tense." Suzie met his eyes.

"If they start throwing punches, I'm putting an end to it." Paul frowned as he sat back down in his chair.

"I think you've got me confused with someone else." The younger man edged away from the older, taller man.

"Oh, I would never forget you." Travis glared at him. "Only a twisted person can make their money off ruining the lives of other people. I don't know what you're doing here in Garber, but I suggest you leave."

"That's enough." Marco Cheney, the owner of the restaurant stepped out from behind the counter. "I won't have this kind of disturbance in my restaurant."

"You shouldn't let people like him in here."

Travis pointed to the man. "Jerome, isn't it? Yeah, I looked you up when you gave those photographs to my ex-wife, I know exactly who you are."

"Travis." The woman at the table stood up and tried to pull him back down into his chair. "Stop this, let's just have our dinner."

"I was just doing my job." Jerome glared at the man, but Suzie noticed a hint of fear in his eyes. "I didn't make you cheat on your wife, did I? I didn't make you lie to her, did I?" He tipped his head towards the woman. "I see it worked out for you, isn't she the one from the pictures?"

The front door of the restaurant swung open, and Detective Jason Allen strode inside. Most of the time Suzie viewed her cousin as a kid, since he was more than twenty years younger than her, but in that moment, he looked every bit the detective that the badge on his belt declared him to be.

"What is all of this about?" Jason stepped between the two men.

"Just a friendly disagreement." Travis took a step back and smiled. "That's all. No need for the law to be involved."

"If that's the case, then it's time for you both to leave." Jason looked between the two men. Briefly he glanced at Suzie and Paul, then returned his attention to the situation at hand.

"Why should I have to leave?" Jerome frowned. "I haven't done anything wrong."

"I got a report of a disturbance. You can refuse to leave if you want, then I will have to open an official investigation into this matter." Jason pulled a notebook from his pocket. "Let's start with your names and your IDs."

"Fine." Jerome waved his hand. "I'll just go." He turned and stalked out of the restaurant.

"Unbelievable, Travis." The woman at his table shook her head. "Ruined your life?" She started towards the door. "Here I thought being free to be with me was a good thing."

"Tess, that's not what I meant." Travis groaned as he followed after her.

"I guess my work here is done." Jason shot a smile in Suzie's direction and snatched a garlic knot from her plate. "Thanks." He nodded to Paul. "You two have a good night. Don't stay out too late."

Suzie rolled her eyes and smiled at him as he left the restaurant.

"He handled that well." Paul cleared his throat. "Although, I don't think that the private investigator should have had to leave. He really didn't do anything wrong."

"And now I know way too much about Travis," Suzie murmured.

After they finished their meal, Suzie walked with Paul back towards the dock.

"How are your new guests?" He glanced over at her.

"They are very easy so far." Suzie smiled and shrugged. "They said they don't want any shared meals, no guided tours. It works for me."

"Sorry our dinner was interrupted with that nonsense." Paul stepped onto the dock. "Hopefully, the two won't encounter each other again."

"What a strange night." Suzie shivered as a cool breeze carried off the surface of the water.

"That guy again." Paul gazed past her, towards the end of the dock, as he wrapped his arm around her shoulders.

"What guy?" Suzie followed his gaze and noticed a stocky man with shoulder length blond hair. He waved his hands through the air as he spoke to a fisherman, Andy, she thought his name was. "The one with Andy?"

"Yes." Paul nodded.

"I think he was at Cheney's tonight, picking up an order."

"I didn't notice him there."

"You were probably distracted by the fight." Suzie shrugged. "He wasn't there for long."

"Before I left for my trip, he was asking me questions about the dock. According to the guys, he's been hanging around the docks the past few days. Asking questions." Paul shrugged, then tightened his grasp around her.

"So, he's curious?" Suzie grinned. "That's your beef with him?"

"My beef?" Paul gazed at her as he smiled. "Yes, that's my beef with him. It's not so much curiosity, as it is nosiness. I don't know. My instincts tell me he's up to something. But then again, I can be a little paranoid." He placed a light kiss on her cheek. "I'm pretty worn out tonight. Can I check in with you in the morning?"

"Sure." Suzie hugged him. "Just glad to have you back on dry land. Have a good night, Paul. Stay away from nosy strangers and angry, cheating husbands."

"I'll do my best." Paul chuckled, gave her a quick kiss, then headed down the dock.

Suzie turned to walk towards Dune House when

she caught sight of a discarded to-go box in the trashcan she walked past. She recognized it as being from Cheney's, and there were even a few garlic knots left in the open box. Her stomach rumbled, despite the fact that she had just eaten.

"Suzie, you have a serious problem." She laughed to herself as she continued down the road towards Dune House. She noticed the light over the porch burned bright. She guessed that Mary was home. She opened the door and stepped inside. The house was quiet and there was no sign of Pilot. Suzie presumed he was nestled in Mary's room for the night. After putting Mary's garlic knots in the refrigerator, she went upstairs. She listened closely but didn't hear Mary's television on in her room. Quietly, she made her way to her room. As she walked past the room that the guests were staying in, she didn't hear anything either. If they were home, they were already sleeping, if not, they had a key to let themselves in. It wasn't until she sprawled out on her bed that she realized how tired she was. Her body sank into the mattress, and her eyes fluttered shut. Her mind jumbled with memories of angry shouts and Paul's light kiss as she fell asleep.

CHAPTER 4

When Suzie woke the next morning, she listened first. As expected, she could hear the coffee brewing, and the soft scuffle of Mary's slippers against the kitchen floor. Her friend almost always woke up before she did. Perhaps it was a leftover habit from being a mother who had to prepare an entire household for the day. Suzie dressed and headed down the stairs to join Mary in the kitchen.

"Morning Mary. How was your night?" She leaned against the counter not far from her friend.

"It was actually pretty amazing." Mary pulled toast from the toaster and put it on a platter. "I hate to say it, but I really liked the place. It really was a homey atmosphere. I thought maybe I would be put off by being so close to so many of the other diners, but I wasn't. In fact, I ended up having a few good conversations. People only had nice things to say about Dune House, too, which was good to hear. And the view is amazing, you can see so many pelicans there. I'm always in awe at how such large birds can glide through the air so easily."

"That does sound nice." Suzie grinned as she gathered two coffee mugs to put on the table. "I had a nice time at Cheney's last night, too. At least until all the drama hit." She rolled her eyes. "Sometimes I think people are just so quick to create a confrontation these days."

"A confrontation?" Mary looked up at her as she buttered the toast. "What kind of confrontation?"

"Nothing too extreme, though it was loud. We were sharing our meal, and out of the blue Travis Parker stood up and began shouting at a diner at another table."

"Travis? The guy that runs the hardware store?" Mary shook her head. "He's never anything but nice to me."

"Me, too." Suzie narrowed her eyes. "But he has been through some trouble lately. I'd heard that he'd recently divorced, but I had no idea why. I found out last night, that's for sure."

"I didn't even know that." Mary sighed. "I'm always behind on the town gossip. Poor guy, divorce is never easy." She carried the tray towards the dining room table.

"Don't feel bad for him just yet." Suzie followed after her with the coffee mugs. "It turns out that the man he yelled at was apparently a private investigator, who Travis' wife hired to investigate Travis. I guess the investigator did a good job and that's what led to the divorce." She set the coffee mugs down on the table. "No wonder Sarah moved out of town. I guess she didn't want to deal with the scandal."

"Wow, I never would have expected that from Travis, he seems like such a nice guy." Mary headed back to the kitchen. "I guess he had a few things to say to the investigator."

"He certainly did. It wasn't until Jason showed up that things finally calmed down and he agreed to leave." Suzie shook her head as she took two plates from Mary to carry to the table. "It wouldn't have surprised me if it had turned into a fist fight, luckily the men restrained themselves. I managed to get Paul to stay out of it, but I'm sure that would have changed if someone had thrown a punch."

"Yes, you're probably right." Mary carried a platter of fresh fruit and yogurt to the table, along with a basket of applesauce muffins. "That should do it for breakfast. I prepared enough for four just in case." She glanced up at the clock. "Though I'm not sure the lovebirds are ever going to come downstairs."

"It's good to see them so involved with each other." Suzie smiled and plucked a strawberry from the platter. As she did, footsteps on the stairs drew her attention to the entrance of the kitchen.

"Good morning." Ginger smiled as she stepped down into the kitchen. "Oh, it smells good in here, and that food looks delicious."

"We'll go out for breakfast." Sam stepped down beside her and caught her elbow. "Let's go get our day started."

Mary's cheeks prickled with a faint sting. She watched as Sam pointedly looked everywhere, but the dining room table.

"Are you sure you wouldn't like an applesauce muffin and some coffee?" Mary got to her feet. "I can get you a cup if you'd like."

"No, thank you." Sam's eyes flicked towards Ginger. "Let's go, we are wasting time."

"He's so eager to get out and explore the town." Ginger smiled and gave his arm a light pat. "We need to get some breakfast in you, so you'll cheer up."

"Enjoy your day." Mary called out to them as they hurried towards the door.

"That was odd, don't you think?" Suzie frowned as she stood up and joined Mary near the kitchen.

"He did say he wanted to handle their meals." Mary shrugged and tore her eyes from the door. "I just thought they would at least want some coffee. Oh well, more for us." She flashed a grin at Suzie. "Up for that trip to the antique store?"

"Sounds good to me." Suzie nodded, then sat back down at the dining room table. "Right after I polish off some of this fruit and yogurt."

"Good idea." Mary eased down into the chair beside Suzie and grabbed a handful of blueberries. As she popped one into her mouth she sat back in her chair and closed her eyes. "So, are you going to try out Pelicans on the Pier?"

"I'm not so sure about it." Suzie shook her head. "It just isn't my style. I'll have to check it out sometime, but I'm not in any rush. I'll clean up, do you want to take Pilot for a walk before we head out?"

"Sure, I can do that." Mary smiled as she finished off the blueberries, then drained her cup of coffee. "Pilot! Walk?"

The Yellow Labrador bolted across the dining room towards Mary.

Mary guided the eager pup towards the sliding glass doors. She clipped on his leash as they stepped outside. At times she let him run free on the beach, but that morning she felt she needed him close by her side. She intended to walk into town. She was curious about where Sam and Ginger might have gone for breakfast. The local café? Or had they gone into Parish in search of a fancy coffee shop?

Pilot tugged her along down the road until he reached a small garden that grew in front of the library. He sniffed at the plants and the grass.

Mary's attention passed between the cars in the parking lot of the library, the nearby diner, and the kids that played on the sidewalk in front of a group of houses. A pang of nostalgia rippled through her as she watched them jump from square to square. Her own children would spend hours playing a similar game. Their laughter still sounded just as fresh in her memory as it did then. A soft bark from Pilot drew her attention back to him.

"Oh, sorry boy, I wandered off in my mind there for a minute, didn't I?" She smiled as she crouched down to pet him. "Let's go to the bakery and get one of those dog cookies. Sound good?"

Pilot's tail flicked back and forth, and he barked again. "I thought so." She grinned and led him towards the bakery. The owner set up a stand outside every morning to give people the opportunity to stop for coffee and a pastry without even having to step into the shop. They also made sure there were plenty of dog treats available for those that walked their dogs in the morning.

"Hello Stacey." Mary smiled at the young woman who stood behind the stand. The owner's daughter, she was barely nineteen, and always had a smile on her face.

"Good morning, Mary, and Pilot." She offered him one of the dog cookies.

"Thanks." Mary handed over a few dollars to pay for the cookie. "He's always so excited to see you."

"Me, too." Stacey gazed at the dog with a warm smile.

"Excuse me." A man stepped up to the stand, his face half-hidden by a baseball cap, but his blond hair peeked out the bottom. "Can I get a coffee, please?"

"Sure. Coming right up." Stacey began to prepare the coffee.

Pilot sniffed at the man's shoes.

"Back off." The man grunted.

"Sorry about that." Mary tugged Pilot away from the man. "He probably smells the fish. Are you a fisherman?"

"I'm just here for a coffee." He shot a brief glance at Mary, then took the coffee from Stacey. He handed her a few dollars, then turned and walked away.

"Do you know him?" Mary looked back at Stacey.

"Not really, no. The past couple of days he shows up, buys a coffee, and goes back to the docks. I tried to chat with him a bit, but he's all business. I don't think he lives around here, though." Stacey shrugged. "Did you hear about what happened at Cheney's last night?" She raised an eyebrow as she smiled. "Crazy, isn't it?"

"I'm not sure what to think of it." Mary frowned. "I'm just glad that things calmed down."

"For the moment. We'd all better hope that Travis doesn't run into that private investigator on the street somewhere." Stacey turned her attention to another customer that stepped up to the cart.

Mary guided Pilot along the sidewalk back towards Dune House. She didn't want to run into Travis, after what she'd learned about him. She did her best not to judge people, but it was hard not to feel that he had betrayed Sarah.

Mary met Suzie at the house, and after settling in Pilot, they left for the antique shop. They spent most of the afternoon looking for the perfect pieces to add to the house. As an amateur interior designer, Suzie had an eye for detail. Mary on the other hand, leaned more towards items that told a story. By the time they returned to Dune House the sun had begun to set. Pilot greeted them eagerly at the door.

"Sorry we were gone so long, buddy." Mary leaned down to pet him. "But we made some great finds."

"We sure did." Suzie grinned as she toted the bags inside the house.

"I'll get us some dinner going." Mary stepped inside the house and headed straight for the kitchen. As she turned on the oven to preheat it, Pilot sprawled out on the floor just outside the kitchen. Mary hummed to herself as she began to put together a small casserole. Just enough for the two of them, since she guessed that their guests already had dinner plans.

Suddenly, Pilot jumped up to his feet. His toenails clicked against the wood floor as he lunged towards the front door. Sharp barks bounced off the walls of the foyer.

"What is it, Pilot?" Mary's stomach lurched as each of Pilot's barks jolted her senses.

"Something's definitely wrong." Suzie hurried into the kitchen at the sound of Pilot's barks.

Mary followed Pilot to the door as her heart pounded. He leaned down and growled, then barked at the door again.

Suzie paused beside Mary. "What is he barking at?"

"I don't know." Mary took a deep breath. Even though she was curious about what might be on the other side of the door, dread also bubbled up into her chest as she reached for the doorknob. The moment she opened the door, the blare of a siren struck her ears.

CHAPTER 5

"Wow, what are all the sirens for?" Suzie stepped out onto the porch and watched as a police car zoomed past, followed by an ambulance.

"Not sure." Mary reached down to pat Pilot's head as he shifted nervously beside her. "Hopefully, it's nothing too serious." She frowned as another police car whipped by.

"It looks like they're headed to the pier, to the new restaurant." Suzie looked over at Mary. "I suggested our guests go there tonight for dinner after your glowing recommendation. I hope they're okay." Suzie clasped her hands together and leaned forward. "Maybe we should take a walk down there and see what's happening."

"Let's take Pilot with. I prefer having him with us in case he gets upset because of the sirens." Mary grabbed Pilot's leash from inside the house. She crouched down and smiled at him as she put it on. "Let's go, buddy. We should check on things." She gave him a light kiss on the top of his head, then stood up.

"I think every police officer in Garber must be there." Suzie started down the front steps. "It must be something major."

"Oh dear." Mary's heart began to pound as she held Pilot's leash tightly. "I hope no one is hurt."

"It's hard to believe that no one is, after that kind of parade of emergency vehicles. But maybe it's some kind of false alarm." Suzie matched her pace as they neared the gathering of emergency vehicles. The bright lights flashed across the sign for Pelicans on the Pier. Several people were gathered outside the restaurant, though corralled within the confines of bright yellow tape that extended out to the edge of the sidewalk in front of the restaurant.

"I don't think it's a false alarm." Mary frowned as she pointed to the coroner's van that was parked not far from the ambulance. "I wonder what happened?"

"I see Ginger and Sam." Suzie pointed at the

couple in the middle of the crowd of people. They clung to each other as they shivered. The night was fairly warm, but many people in the crowd trembled.

"There's Louis, too." Mary pointed out the librarian that they had become good friends with since they had moved to Garber.

With Pilot close behind them, the pair picked their way through the crowd of onlookers towards Louis.

"Louis, what's going on?" Suzie paused beside him, just outside of the tape.

"Suzie, don't get too close." Louis took a step back. "They don't know what caused it yet."

"Caused what?" Suzie's heart skipped a beat as she took the step back that Louis recommended.

"Someone died in the restaurant." Louis shuddered. "He just stood up from the table and started foaming at the mouth. I've never seen anything like it. I've read about it of course. It could be a sign of poisoning." He frowned as he looked in the direction of the ambulance. "We all have to wait here until we've been evaluated, and then we'll be interviewed by the police. It's going to be a long night."

Mary's eyes swept over the crowd of people. If someone had been poisoned in the family-style dining restaurant, it was likely that many other people had eaten the same tainted food. Yet everyone in the crowd appeared to be healthy, shaken, but healthy.

"I'm so sorry that you witnessed that, Louis." Suzie frowned as she met his eyes. "Is there anything I can do to help."

"Just tell me it's crazy to think that I'll be next." Louis ran his hand back through his hair as he took a deep breath. "I'm trying not to lose my mind over this."

"It's all right, Louis." Suzie looked straight into his eyes. "If you were poisoned, you would be showing signs of it already. You would already be at the hospital if the paramedics suspected that others might have been poisoned. I think what happened to the diner was something that happened only to him." She reached across the yellow tape and offered him her hand. "You're going to be just fine. I promise."

Louis blinked back tears as he took her hand. "Thank you, Suzie." He took another deep breath. "That's what I needed to hear. Logically, I know it's true, but after seeing what I did, I think I'm just being paranoid."

"Do you know who it was?" Mary stepped closer to the tape as well. "Was it a local?"

"No, it wasn't. It was someone from out of town. I wasn't sitting too close to him, but it was a man, in his late twenties or early thirties. Way too young to die." Louis grimaced. "Not that there is ever a right age. I just wish we could all go home. Keeping us roped up like this is even more panic-inducing."

"Let me see if I can find Jason." Suzie gave his hand a squeeze. "Maybe we can get things moving along."

"Do you think I should go say something to Ginger and Sam?" Mary looked in their direction. They seemed isolated from the other people gathered together, who were mostly locals.

"Let me talk to Jason first." Suzie pointed to a group of police officers that surrounded one man in particular. "I'm sure he'll give me an update on the situation, then we'll at least have something to tell them."

"Good idea." Mary followed along behind her as Suzie approached the crowd of officers. Most wore Garber Police Department uniforms, but Mary noticed that some wore Parish Police Department uniforms. "They must have called in help from Parish." Mary skimmed the group in search of one particular face. If Wes was present, he wasn't in the tangle of officers.

Jason stood in the middle of the group, his head bent over a clipboard in his hand.

"We need to get these people processed so that they can be on their way. Make sure that each one has been checked by a medic. I've been told they have, but I want a second confirmation from each of them before they are questioned." Jason looked up at the officers. "Understand that? I don't want anyone questioned until they have been medically cleared. Once you interview them, if there's anyone you think I need to speak with, pass that information on to me, if not, make sure you have their correct contact information and you can release them." He tapped his fingertip on the clipboard. "We have a lot of people here, and one mistake could mean life or death in this case. Do not cut any corners. Any problems, report them to me immediately." He nodded to the officers. "Go ahead and get started."

As the officers began to filter through the crowd of people waiting, Suzie walked up to Jason.

"Excuse me, Jason, I know you're busy, but my guests are part of your group that you're questioning. Do you think you could give me an idea of what's going on?" She met his eyes as he glanced up at her.

"Suzie." Jason looked past her, then nodded to Mary. As he looked back at Suzie his eyes narrowed. "I don't have much time to spare. As it looks now, a man was poisoned while eating at the restaurant. However, at this point we can't be certain of that. He may have not been poisoned and died from something else. He may have been poisoned before he ever arrived. So far there haven't been any signs of anyone else being poisoned, which is both a good thing and a puzzling thing, since they were all sharing the same food. We're working on finding out what he ingested that was poisoned. Summer suspects that the poison was ingested, but it's just a suspicion until she can complete tests and an autopsy. As of now, we're asking everyone who was present to submit to a medical exam and an interview. After that, they will be free to go." He lowered his clipboard to his side. "This is a big mess, Suzie, they're just going to have to be patient."

"I understand." Suzie frowned as she peered through the front door of the restaurant. "Do you know who the victim was? Louis said it was someone from out of town."

Jason lowered his voice. "It was the man from Cheney's last night. Jerome Poole."

"Seriously?" Suzie's eyes widened. "The private investigator?"

"We're still looking into that." Jason wiped his hand across his forehead. "I have a feeling there are going to be a lot of pieces to this puzzle." He glanced up as an officer called to him. "I'm sorry, I have to go."

Mary watched Jason walk away. She stepped closer to Suzie.

"If it was Jerome, do you think that Travis had something to do with it? You said they fought last night, right?" She bit into her bottom lip.

"I hate to think it, but yes it's certainly possible." Suzie scanned the crowd of people gathered behind the police tape. "I don't see him, though. If he was in the restaurant, he wasn't a diner."

"Or he slipped out before the police arrived." Mary's heart pounded at the thought. "It seems so extreme to poison someone." She narrowed her eyes. "That's something that a restaurant can't recover from. No matter what the truth turns out to be, Pelicans on the Pier won't be a place that people want to dine at anymore."

"That's an interesting point." Suzie glanced

over at her with a raised eyebrow. "Maybe, Jerome was just a victim of circumstances. Maybe the point was to deal a blow to Pelicans on the Pier and force it to close. Not everyone is welcoming to new businesses around here, remember?"

"Yes, we had a few rough patches when we first opened, but no one poisoned us. Who would want to do that?" Mary crossed her arms, then her eyes widened. "Do you mean you think someone at Cheney's might have had something to do with this?"

"I don't know what to think just yet." Suzie shook her head. "But we can't rule anything out. My guess is that Travis wasn't the only person that Jerome made an enemy out of due to his line of work. The police are going to have a long list of suspects to work through."

"This is going to be a scandal for the whole town." Mary looked over at Sam and Ginger as they spoke to one of the officers. "I'm sure this is not the weekend away that they were hoping for."

"You're right about that." Suzie took a deep breath. "I'll be surprised if they don't check out tonight."

"Maybe we should offer them a free night?"

Mary frowned. "It might at least boost our chances of still getting a good review."

"That's not a bad idea. It isn't fair that their vacation has been ruined by this. I'll offer it to them when they get back." Suzie turned back towards the crowd of people. "I just hope that no one else was harmed by this."

"I think if they were, we would know by now." Mary's mind swirled as the sirens from new police cars jostled her thoughts. She took a deep breath of the crisp night air. "I think I need to head back, Suzie. I need a break from this, and I think I should get Pilot home."

"I'm right there with you." Suzie slipped her arm through the warm crook of Mary's elbow. "There's nothing we can do here right now, anyway. It looks like Louis is being interviewed, so he should be released soon. It would be better to get back and have some tea and snacks waiting for Sam and Ginger. Who knows if they were able to finish their dinner."

"Let's hope they didn't." Mary winced.

CHAPTER 6

O nce back home and Pilot was happily chewing on a bone, Mary prepared an assortment of snacks and some hot tea.

Suzie set the silver cream and sugar tray down on the wooden dining room table, just as the front door opened.

"Sam, Ginger." Suzie straightened up.

Mary hurried from the kitchen to join her in the foyer.

"Are you both okay?" She watched as they undid their jackets and hung them on the pegs on the wall.

"We're fine." Ginger smiled, though not nearly as wide as normal. "It wasn't an easy night, though."

"We heard." Suzie clasped her hands together. "We thought you might like some tea and snacks."

"Actually, we just want to go to bed." Sam's shoulder brushed against Suzie's as he stepped past her.

"I understand." Suzie walked after him. "But I did want to offer you both an extra night, free of charge." She glanced back at Ginger, who had accepted a hug from Mary. "I know this evening couldn't have been a good experience for you, and we thought you might like to have another day to enjoy yourselves."

"That's wonderful." Ginger met Suzie's eyes. "How kind of you."

"Ginger, it's better if we leave tomorrow, just like we planned." Sam frowned. He tapped his foot beside the entrance to the stairway in the kitchen.

"Sam, relax. We planned an extra day off to recover from our vacation. Instead we can use it to enjoy one more day here, how can you turn that down?" Ginger smiled.

"Maybe because I just watched a man die, poisoned by the food he ate, here in this town." Sam narrowed his eyes. "Sorry, but that doesn't sound like a good vacation to me."

"Sam." Ginger joined him at the bottom of the stairs. "There's no need to be rude."

"He's not wrong." Suzie joined them in the kitchen, with Mary right behind her.

"It had to be terrible." Mary nodded, as inwardly her chest tightened. "We completely understand if you don't want to stay, but I can assure you, we have eaten at all of the restaurants around here, and nothing like this has ever happened to us."

"Maybe it didn't happen to you, but it sure did happen to Jerome." Sam tipped his head towards the stairs. "I'm going to bed, Ginger. If you want to stay here, that's your choice." Sam's shoes struck each step heavily as he climbed.

"I'm sorry, I'm sure he'll feel a little better in the morning." Ginger's cheeks flushed. "We'd love to stay another night, thank you." She turned and followed her husband up the stairs.

"Interesting." Suzie smiled as she turned back to face Mary.

"Sam's attitude?" Mary shook her head. "I know he's been through a shock, but he's just so gruff."

"No, I meant, it's interesting that Ginger decided to accept our offer, even when Sam didn't want to. With his attitude, I thought maybe he liked to be in charge, but it seems to me that Ginger is the one who calls the shots." Suzie helped Mary clean up and put away the snacks she'd prepared.

"They do seem to have a very interesting dynamic in their relationship. Did you notice that Sam called Jerome by name?" Mary raised an eyebrow. "Do you think they got to know each other over dinner?"

"I'm not sure." Suzie set the last dish in the sink.

A knock on the front door made Mary jump.

"Who could that be?" She glanced at the clock. "Well, I guess it's not as late as I thought."

"I'll go check." Suzie walked up to the door, then peeked through the window beside it. "It's Jason." She pulled the door open and waved him inside.

"Thanks." Jason pulled his hat off as he stepped in. "I just wanted to stop in and see if everything was all right here." He looked between them and clutched his hat in his hands. "Are your guests sleeping?"

"Yes, they are." Mary led him towards the kitchen. "Would you like some tea? I just made it."

"Sure. My nerves could certainly use some. Thanks." Jason leaned against the counter as she poured him a cup of tea. "How are your guests?"

"They were shaken up, but we offered them a

free night, and I think that helped." Mary handed him the tea. "I'm sure a quick police response helped, too."

"I appreciate that." Jason smiled, but the expression faded quickly. "Are you aware of what Ginger does for a living?" He ran his fingertips along the brim of his hat.

"Not really, no." Mary shrugged as she gazed at him.

"She is a scientist. A chemist. She develops medications. In fact, it's possible she's worked with the very same compound that is suspected to have killed Jerome. It's not an uncommon substance, but it's also not something that you can just buy off the shelf. I need to speak to her about it." Jason tilted his head to the side. "I think there may be a connection there."

"With Ginger?" Mary took a sharp breath, then covered her mouth.

"Jason, are you serious?" Suzie stared at him. "You think she had something to do with it?"

"I didn't say that." Jason sighed and glanced towards the stairs that led from the kitchen to the guest rooms. "I'd appreciate if you both don't allude to the idea that I suspect her. I'd rather she stick around long enough for me to talk to her again. I just find it interesting that she happened to be in the restaurant, when it looks like it's possible she worked with the same substance that likely poisoned Jerome."

"We won't say anything." Suzie crossed her arms. "But Sam sounded eager to leave. I'm not sure that they will stay the extra night."

"I understand. I don't have a motive yet, but I think the connection warrants a little more investigation. I'll do as much digging as I can tonight."

"So, you didn't arrest anyone at the restaurant?" Mary studied the creases in his face. They seemed to tighten each time she or Suzie spoke. "No initial suspects?"

"Yes, we have the chef in custody. But that is just so we can question him on a few things. He does have a record of assault and attempted murder." Jason sipped his tea.

"Really?" Mary's eyes widened. "Are you saying that Wes and I ate at a restaurant where the chef is an attempted murderer?"

"It's more common than you might think. Many criminals don't have a lot of options once they have a felony on their record. Restaurants can be pretty lax in their background checks." Jason took another swallow of the tea. "I've read over his file. I'm not so sure that his guilt was actually proven, but I wasn't the investigator on the case. Either way, it makes him a prime suspect, I'm just not ready to believe that he should be the only suspect. Thanks for this." He held up his tea cup. "Do you mind if I take it to go?"

"Of course not." Mary smiled and gave his shoulder a pat. She grabbed a paper cup from a stack they kept for their guests and transferred the tea into it. "Jason, if there's anything Suzie and I can do to help with the investigation, just let us know."

"Do your best to get Sam and Ginger to stay the extra night." Jason took the paper cup from her. "I'd rather not have to force them to stay."

"We'll do what we can." Suzie nodded, then watched as he stepped through the door. "What a tough night."

"Very." Mary frowned as she crossed her arms. "I can't help but be a little concerned about what he said, though. Do you think that there's any chance that Ginger could be involved?"

"I don't see how." Suzie glanced towards the stairs. "But if there is a connection, I'm sure that Jason will find it. No matter what, I think we all need a good night's sleep." She started towards the stairs. "I'll see you in the morning, Mary."

"Good night, Suzie." Mary started towards her room, and Pilot bounded right after her.

As Suzie reached her room, she heard hushed voices in the guest room. She paused. Normally, she respected her guests' privacy. But she couldn't get her feet to move forward, or her ears to stop listening to the muffled words.

"Do you think it's wise to stay?" Sam's voice drifted through the door.

"I think it's fine. It can't hurt anything." Ginger responded in a slightly louder tone.

"That's what you said about this entire idea."

"And everything is fine. If you would just relax, it would be even better."

"I never should have agreed to this." Sam's voice rose.

Suzie jumped as she saw the doorknob begin to turn. She hurried across the hall to her room and managed to close the door just before she heard the guest room door swing open.

"I'm going to get some extra towels," Ginger said. "Then we can have a shower to relax and try to get some rest. Everything will look so much brighter in the morning."

Suzie pressed her forehead against the cool surface of the door as Ginger's optimism washed over her. It was easy to believe that someone as cheerful as her could never hurt anyone, but from that conversation she had to wonder what exactly had driven them to be in Garber, and at Pelicans on the Pier, on the same night that Jerome was killed. Maybe Jason's suspicions weren't so off base.

CHAPTER 7

*S*uzie settled in her bed with her computer and began to conduct some searches about Jerome. After just about an hour of attempts she realized she wasn't going to get very far. As a private investigator Jerome was good at cleaning up his tracks. She found his name mentioned on a few sites, but only to describe his business, nothing personal. She couldn't even pin down where he went to high school to find any family information about him. Frustrated, she shifted gears and focused on Ginger and Sam instead.

As Suzie conducted a search on their address, she discovered that it didn't belong to an actual house. Instead it was the address of a company. Curious, she searched a little further and found a social media profile for Ginger. It was her picture on the profile, however the profile's privacy settings didn't allow her to view any more information about Ginger. She finally gave up and set her computer on the bedside table. Maybe Ginger had a positive attitude, but apparently, she also had a few secrets. She turned out the light and closed her eyes. The moment she did she recalled the look in Jerome's eyes as Travis turned on him in the restaurant. He was afraid. Did he have reason to be? Did Travis decide to finish the job? Her mind refused to allow her to rest.

By the time Suzie was too exhausted to keep her eyes open, she'd journeyed down several possible paths of how the murder might have happened. However, the last thought that crossed her mind was Marco Cheney. How upset was he that he didn't get the building on the pier? What was he willing to do to prevent the loss of his business to a new restaurant?

Suzie woke up later than usual the next morning, likely due to her mind launching into full investigative mode the night before. As she pulled herself out of bed, the aroma of coffee tickled her nostrils. Mary was already up. Did that mean that Sam and Ginger were, too? She recalled the conversation she'd overheard the night before, and instantly she worried about Mary being alone with the two of them. If they had planned this, then maybe they didn't plan to stop with just one victim. She threw on her robe and hurried down the stairs into the kitchen.

"Suzie." Mary gave a short gasp and laughed. "You startled me. You came down those stairs so fast."

"Where are Ginger and Sam?" Suzie peeked into the dining room. "Have you seen them yet this morning?"

"No, I haven't seen them. They were gone before I got up." Mary shook her head. "I'm not sure how that's possible, but they did leave a note saying that they would take the extra night." Mary poured Suzie a cup of coffee. "Are you doing okay? You look exhausted."

"I didn't get much sleep last night." Suzie shook her head as the coffee mug warmed her palms. "I heard them talking before I went to bed." She shared with Mary what she could remember of the conversation as Pilot came over for a cuddle.

"That does sound pretty incriminating. It's certainly not an admission of guilt, but they are definitely up to something." Mary leaned back against the counter.

"Yes, and I found out that the address they gave us is bogus. It belongs to a business. Why would they give us a fake address?" Suzie took a sip of her coffee. She closed her eyes as the hot liquid singed the surface of her tongue.

"That's pretty suspicious, too." Mary shifted closer to Suzie. "I guess we should tell Jason about it."

"Yes, I think we should." Suzie pulled her phone out of her pocket. "I'll give him a call."

"Don't bother." Mary tipped her head towards the window that overlooked the parking lot. "He just pulled in."

Mary met Jason at the door and opened it for him.

"Good morning, Jason."

"Good morning, Mary." He pulled his hat off and frowned.

"My, you look worse than your cousin." Mary frowned as she studied the dark circles under his eyes and his ruffled red hair. "Did you get any sleep last night?"

"No." Jason looked past her, to Suzie. "I need to speak with Sam and Ginger."

"I'm sorry, Jason, but they've already gone out." Suzie shrugged. "They said they would stay the extra night, though. They were gone before Mary got up this morning."

"Interesting." Jason sighed. "I guess I'll have to wait until later to speak to them."

"Jason, I did learn a few things about them." Suzie filled him in on what she had overheard, and her search on their address.

"Yes, their address is part of the reason I'm here. They gave a fake address to one of the patrol officers. It might have been the same one they gave you." Jason sniffed the air. "Is that coffee?"

"Sure, let me get you a cup." Suzie walked back towards the kitchen.

"How are you holding up, Mary?" Jason looked over at her.

"That's so sweet of you to ask, when you're the one under so much stress." Mary led him into the dining room. "I'm fine I suppose."

"I know you ate at the restaurant the night before Jerome died. I just want you to know that there haven't been any other reports of sickness from anyone that ate there since it opened." Jason looked into her eyes. "You have nothing to worry about."

"You know what's strange? I hadn't even thought about that." Mary settled in one of the chairs at the table. "I've been so caught up in what happened to Jerome that I hadn't really considered that anyone else that ate at the restaurant previously could be at risk, including myself."

"As it looks right now, Jerome was the only one poisoned. The restaurant is going to remain closed for the time being." Jason set his notepad on the table between them as Suzie returned with a cup of coffee and the cream and sugar tray.

"I had a terrible time keeping Marco Cheney off my mind last night." Suzie sat down across from him. "Do you think he might have had anything to do with this?"

"Actually, the Cheneys have an alibi. They were both at the restaurant last night at the time of the murder, with plenty of witnesses to prove it." Jason spooned some sugar into his coffee. "However, that doesn't clear them completely."

"It doesn't?" Mary looked over at him. "How is that possible?"

"Although they may not have been the ones to put the poison into the victim's food, there was someone at the restaurant that could have been acting on their behalf." He pulled out his phone and displayed a picture of a man. "This is Chef Cody Shouder. He was recently hired by Pelicans on the Pier. Only about a week after he was fired from his job at Cheney's."

"Really?" Suzie's eyes widened. "I've seen him around town, I've spoken to him a couple of times. I've never really paid attention to who the chef was there. So, he was fired from Cheney's and went to Pelicans on the Pier? Why would he want to poison Jerome if it meant possibly losing his job?" She crossed her arms. Then before Jason could answer she snapped her fingers and spoke in a rush. "Because you think the termination was a ruse, and that Shouder applied for the job at the Cheneys' request."

"I think it's possible." Jason nodded, then kicked the sole of his shoe along the wooden floor beneath him. "It's certainly a stretch, but at this point I can't rule it out. I imagine that having one of their longtime employees infiltrate the new restaurant would have given them the upper hand."

"But if they had that upper hand already, why would they push it to murder?" Mary shook her head slowly. "They already had an inside man that could cause any kind of destruction they chose.

Why would they jump straight to murder? The Cheneys don't seem like murderers to me."

"Maybe not, but Jason has a point. There is a connection between the chef and the Cheneys, it has to be investigated. It's too much of a coincidence to ignore." Suzie took a sip of her coffee.

"True, but let's say they did instruct the chef to do it, why would they, or he, target an innocent customer? Why not go after the staff?" Mary tapped her fingertips against the table. "It doesn't add up to me."

"You're right, it doesn't make much sense. But at the moment not much about the crime makes sense. It's possible that Shouder didn't realize how much he put in. Maybe he intended to only make a customer sick, to get the new restaurant some bad reviews. But I'll be honest, I don't think there's much chance the Cheneys were involved in this. Still, I have to follow up on any leads." Jason took a big swallow of his coffee.

"Any updates on the autopsy?" Mary pushed a plate of muffins towards him.

"Yes, Summer was able to confirm that the poison we suspected was the poison that the victim ingested. She also determined that the poison was mixed into something he ate, not drank. So, we are leaning on the chef even more." Jason smiled as he took one of the muffins. "Thanks."

"I don't understand. How could it be on something that he ate? Wouldn't everyone else at his table be poisoned as well?" Mary shook her head.

"We're still trying to figure that out. That's the only update I have for you right now." He took one last drink from his mug of coffee. "I should get going. Please let me know if you see or hear from Sam and Ginger. I'd really like to speak to them as soon as possible, and they're not answering their phones."

"Yes, of course, we'll let you know." Suzie walked him to the door. "Jason, make sure you get some rest at some point."

"I will. At some point." Jason raised an eyebrow, then headed out the door.

"What a tragedy." Mary stood up from the table. "To think, everyone was there to just have a good night and enjoy a meal. Instead it ended in something terrible."

"You're right, Mary, but you also made me realize something. To find out what happened in that restaurant last night, we need to talk to someone who was actually there. Someone who handled the food and knows how the kitchen operates." Suzie's lips tightened as she stared straight at her friend. "We need to speak to someone on the waitstaff. If the poison was only in Jerome's food, then someone sitting close to him, or someone who served him the food, had to be the one to poison it."

"That's true." Mary frowned. "Although it could still have been the chef."

"Maybe, but we won't get to speak with him for quite some time, if at all. Jason needs our help with this whether he knows it or not. We need to figure out if Sam and Ginger had something to do with this before they decide to leave." Suzie grabbed her keys from the hook near the door. "Do you remember who waited on you when you and Wes ate at Pelicans on the Pier?"

"Yes, it was a young man named Sean." Mary watched as Suzie began to head for the door. "Suzie, you're still in your robe."

"I am?" Suzie looked down at her tightly knotted robe. "Oh, well, I guess I'd better change." She huffed and headed for the stairs.

"I'll see if I can find Sean's address." Mary covered her mouth, but Suzie could still hear her laugh.

"No comments, Mary." Suzie shouted from the top of the stairs.

Mary managed to get Sean's full name and address by calling Louis the librarian. He knew just about everyone in Garber. She sent a text with the details to Suzie.

After she changed, Suzie hurried back down the steps and towards the front door. She bent down to pat Pilot on the way out.

"Mary, please let me know if you hear from our guests."

"I will." Mary called out to her, then grabbed Pilot by the collar. He barked and attempted to follow Suzie out the door. "Don't worry, pal, she's going to be just fine."

Suzie pushed the door closed behind her, then walked over to her car. She hoped that a conversation with Sean would give her some direction as to who might have actually put the poison in Jerome's food. As she drove to his address, she prepared herself for what she might find. Could the waiter be a hardened killer?

CHAPTER 8

Suzie parked in front of Sean's house, and walked up the thin sidewalk that led to the front porch. She heard the swish of a broom against wooden planks and looked up to see a young man in the act of sweeping. To her surprise she recognized him. He had spent some time working with Paul on his boat, and Paul had mentored him when he showed interest in becoming a fisherman.

"Hi Sean." She smiled as she stepped up onto the small, front porch.

"Hi." Sean leaned on the broom he gripped in his hands. "Suzie, right?"

"Right." Suzie nodded as she glanced around the porch. It needed some repairs, but it appeared sturdy, just like the house it was attached to. "How are you today?"

"All right, I guess." Sean set the broom against the wall, then turned back to face her. "Can I help you with something?"

"I heard that you were working at Pelicans on the Pier last night." Suzie clutched her hands together.

"Yes, I was." His eyes darted towards the front door of the house, then back to Suzie. "Try to keep your voice down, all right?"

"Is something wrong?" Suzie looked towards the door as well.

"It's my mom. She's not well, her heart." Sean tapped his chest. "If she heard about what happened last night, I think it might put her in the hospital. I've been trying to keep her out of it."

"I'm sorry." Suzie softened her voice, then gestured to the front walkway. "Would you like to go for a walk and talk about it? I know that you must have some things on your mind."

"I do." Sean nodded, then glanced once more at the door. "Just a short walk, though."

"Of course." Suzie smiled as she descended the steps.

As he fell into step beside her, an awkward

silence rippled between them. Suzie was aware of just how vulnerable he was, perhaps not even twenty yet, and a caregiver to his sick mother. She didn't want to push him too hard. Yet, she also knew that he was the one who might hold the key to solving Jerome's murder.

"How are you holding up, Sean?" Suzie glanced over at him.

"All right I guess." He kicked a small stone on the sidewalk and watched it skip across the pavement. "I tried to help him, you know? But I didn't know how. It wasn't like he was choking. If he was choking, I would have been able to help him."

"I don't think there was anything you could have done." Suzie lightly touched his arm. "I don't think there was anything anyone could have done."

"The police, they keep telling me that I should remember things. That I should know things. But all I can see when I think about last night, is the way he stumbled away from the table." Sean stopped walking and closed his eyes.

"I'm so sorry, Sean. I can only imagine how overwhelming that is for you." As much as Suzie wanted to comfort him, she also wanted the answers that he hadn't been able to give to the police. "You know sometimes when we have an upsetting experience, our minds hyperfocus on only that part of our memory. It makes all the other memories around it get jumbled up."

"Yes, it's just like that." Sean nodded. "I know I should remember what he ordered. I know that I should remember talking to him. But all I can remember is what happened after he ate."

"You can remember more. You just have to try and relax, do your best to keep yourself calm." Suzie turned to look at him. "I might be able to help you with it, if you'd like me to." She had used relaxation techniques many times when she was an investigative journalist.

"Yes, I think I would." Sean balled his hands into fists. "The police, they keep hounding me, and I want to help them, I really do, but I think they're starting to suspect me. I didn't do anything to hurt that man. You believe me, don't you, Suzie?"

"Yes, I do." Suzie smiled as she led him to a nearby bench. "Just sit down here, and I'll walk you through it. All right?"

"Yes." Sean sat down on the bench. "What do I do?"

"Close your eyes. Try to relax. Just listen to the sound of my voice." Suzie did her best to sound soothing as she walked him through a few relaxation exercises. She noticed the tension begin to leave his face, and then his body. When she thought he was as relaxed as she could get him to be, she tried to guide him through the memories. "Now, I want you to think about showing up for work yesterday. Just when you first got there. Can you tell me anything about that? Did you speak to anyone?"

"Yes." Sean smiled some. "I spoke to Cassie."

"And who is Cassie?" Suzie sat down on the bench beside him.

"She's a waitress." Sean's voice went up an octave.

"Is she your friend?" Suzie smiled.

"I'd like her to be more than that, but I haven't been able to ask her out, yet." Sean smiled as well.

"How do you feel when you see Cassie?" Suzie leaned a little closer to him.

"Happy, a little nervous, just glad to be around her." Sean shrugged.

"Okay, I want you to remember how you feel when you see her. Remember that. Now, I want you to tell me, what was the dinner rush like? Was it busy?" Suzie shifted some on the bench, careful not to touch him.

"It was crazy. Lots more people than we

expected. The chef was getting pretty angry." Sean's lips tensed.

"Where is Justine?"

"She's on the other side of the restaurant." Sean smiled. "She is so quick, back and forth to the kitchen."

"And where is Cassie? What is she doing?" Suzie bit into her bottom lip. She hoped that he wouldn't come out of his relaxed state before he could answer her.

"She's laughing. She doesn't let anything get to her. She's got one of the big tables. She's joking with them. They're not mad, even though they have to wait for their food. She's really good at her job." Sean smiled.

"And you? What is your table like?" Suzie held her breath.

"There are a lot of people that don't know each other. I can tell because they're not talking much. I'm still taking their orders, and some people are getting impatient." Sean frowned.

"Who was the most impatient? Was there someone at the table who upset you?" Suzie pulled her phone out to take notes.

"A couple. They have a lot of demands. They want to make sure there is no pepper in the mushroom gravy." Sean shook his head. "They're not from around here."

"I see." Suzie nodded as she imagined they might be Ginger and Sam. "What kind of orders are you taking?"

"Just drinks. Mostly. Except for one man." Sean took a sharp breath.

"And where is Cassie? Did she get her food for her table, yet?" Suzie's heart skipped a beat. She sensed that he was about to lose his focus.

"She's almost to the kitchen, but one of the people at my table calls out to her. They're not supposed to do that, I'm their waiter. But he calls out to her, he wants a glass of wine. What he needs is a haircut." Sean chuckled. "But Cassie just smiles and says she will bring it right out. I feel like it's my fault because I'm not moving fast enough. But this guy is taking forever to give me his order. He wants an extra side, just for himself. Mashed potatoes, with no butter." He cringed. "Who wants to eat that? I offer him some sour cream. He insists he just wants the potatoes, no butter."

"And do you remember who this was? The one that ordered the mashed potatoes?" Suzie's muscles tensed in anticipation.

"It's Jerome. He's the only one that ordered

them with no butter. The chef will have to make him his own bowl. He's not going to be happy. He's already mad." Sean's breathing grew sharper.

"Okay Sean. Is Cassie back with the other man's wine?" Suzie placed her hand lightly on his. Her fingertips grazed across the sheen of sweat on his palm. She looked up at his face and noticed the tension in his facial muscles. "Did the chef yell at you, Sean?"

"He threw a pan at me. He told me to get out of his kitchen." Sean frowned. "I don't know if he's going to make the special order of mashed potatoes or not. I don't know if I'll ever be good at this job. Not like Cassie is."

"Where is she?" Suzie softened her voice. "Can you see her?"

"She's handing me the glass of wine. She pinches my cheek and winks at me and tells me it will all be over soon." Sean smiled. "She makes this job so worth it." He opened his eyes. "I remembered, didn't I?"

"Yes, you did, Sean. You did good." Suzie smiled, as she gave his hand a light pat. "You should tell the police what you remember." She stood up from the bench. "And by the way, now would be the perfect time to ask Cassie out." She met his eyes. "Maybe she likes you, too."

"I don't know?" Sean stood up as well. "I'm still so nervous to ask her."

"Just remember how she makes you feel. It'll be worth it to take the risk, don't you think? You'll never know unless you ask." Suzie turned to walk back towards her car.

"You're right. It is worth it. Thanks Suzie." Sean waved to her as he climbed the steps to his front porch.

Suzie waved to him, then dialed Jason's number on her phone.

"Hi Suzie, I can't talk right now, I'm in the middle of something."

"Jason, it was mashed potatoes. Jerome had his own bowl of mashed potatoes without butter. No one else would have been eating them. My guess is the poison was in the mashed potatoes." Suzie glanced back at Sean who stepped into his house and closed the door. "Sean told me."

"Sean the waiter? We couldn't get two words out of him." Jason's voice deepened. "Are you sure?"

"I'm sure. Have Summer test the mashed potatoes

that were in a bowl beside Jerome's chair. I know everyone had mashed potatoes, so maybe she only tested the main dish. But his were made separately for him, he didn't want any butter in them." Suzie started her car. "Please, let me know what you find, Jason."

"Will do." Jason ended the call.

CHAPTER 9

When Suzie parked in front of Dune House, she felt some relief that Sean had managed to remember an important detail, but it didn't exactly make everything crystal clear. She hoped that Mary would be able to discern something from the information that would move things along.

Pilot greeted her at the door with Mary only a few steps behind.

"Did you find him?" Mary gave Pilot's side a light pat.

"Yes, I did." Suzie led her to the dining room table then filled her in on her conversation with Sean.

"So, if the poison was in the mashed potatoes,

there's a good chance that the chef is the one who put the poison in them." Mary tapped her fingertips on the table top. "Did Sean remember anything else?"

"I think he might have if I kept pushing him, but he'd already said so much I thought it was best to stop and let him come to terms with what he remembered first. Sometimes you can push too hard if it's an upsetting experience. Maybe if he'd be willing to talk with me again, I could find out more." Suzie crossed her arms as she stared out over the water. "He did mention that there was a couple that were quite difficult diners. I think it was Sam and Ginger." She flashed a smile in Mary's direction.

"I can understand that." Mary laughed. "I'm still a little hurt by their avoidance of my applesauce muffins."

"There's something else that Sean said that has been bugging me." Suzie sat back in her chair and closed her eyes as she recalled his words. "He said that the chef threw a pan at him. He was so frustrated with the workload that he got furious when Sean asked for the extra serving of mashed potatoes."

"All the more reason that he might have decided to poison them." Mary scooted her chair closer to

Suzie's. "Maybe he'd had enough. Maybe he snapped. He might not have even been targeting Jerome."

"Yes, it's possible that he snapped, that it all became too much. But poisoning someone isn't something that you just do on a whim. It's something you plan. He wouldn't have just had the poison lying around. Would he? As angry as he was, I could imagine him spitting in the food, or something awful like that. But not deciding to pour some poison into it. That's an extreme reaction to frustration." Suzie folded her hands on the table and took a deep breath. "I really think that if he was in that mental state, it makes him less likely of a suspect."

"You're right it would be odd for him to have the poison. But maybe he was already planning to poison someone, and Jerome just happened to win the lottery since he was the one that asked for extra potatoes." The legs of Mary's chair scraped across the wooden floor as she pushed it back and stood up. She gripped the edge of the table to steady herself and clenched her teeth.

Pilot nudged her hand with his head. He looked up at her with wide eyes.

"It's okay, boy." Mary smiled at him as she stroked his head.

"I think he can tell that your knees are bothering you." Suzie frowned. "Is the medicine not helping anymore?"

"I try not to take too much of it." Mary cleared her throat. "Do you think the chef might have planned this ahead of time?"

"That is definitely possible, but I'm not sure that it adds up for me. If he planned to poison someone last night, then why was he so stressed over getting the food prepared? Why did he care if he was doing a good job or not? And why just one person?" Suzie frowned. "If someone does something like that, don't they want to make a big splash and get lots of attention?"

"That's a good question. It's probably best answered by the man himself." Mary reached down to pet Pilot. "Any chance that Jason will let us speak to him?"

"I doubt it. He's their prime suspect and he's keeping him under lock and key." Suzie raised an eyebrow. "But there might be someone else we can speak to, to get a better idea of exactly how the poison was put into the food, and what kind of poison it was. Why don't we meet Summer for lunch?"

"Do you think she'll be free?" Mary gave Pilot a treat.

"Only one way to find out." Suzie pulled out her phone and dialed Summer's number. After three rings, Summer answered.

"Suzie, I was wondering when I would hear from you." Her voice wavered with amusement.

"Would you like to meet for lunch?" Suzie smiled.

"Sure. I can be at the diner in thirty. I could use a break from all of this." Summer ended the call.

"We have a lunch date, Mary." Suzie stood up and clipped Pilot's leash on. "I'll take Pilot for a quick walk, then we can head over to the diner."

"Great." Mary grabbed her phone as it rang. "Hello?" She paused, then nodded. "Yes, I'll put some in your room." She ended the call. "That was Ginger, she wanted to know if she can have some more shampoo, or if she needed to buy some. I guess they are definitely still planning to stay."

"That's good news." Suzie smiled as she led Pilot out through the sliding glass doors.

*M*ary pulled open the door to the diner and held it for Suzie so that she could walk through. Familiar smells greeted her, a bit of grease, a bit of ketchup, and the air freshener that pumped out tiny bursts of flowery scents. She crinkled up her nose and held her breath.

"There she is." Suzie grabbed Mary's hand and led her to a table where the medical examiner, Jason's wife, sat. "Hi Summer."

"I ordered us some chicken fingers and fries." Summer stood up and hugged each of them, then settled back in her chair. "Sorry, I'm starving, and I know that you both like them."

"It's perfect, thanks." Mary sat down across from her. "I'm guessing this is the first break you've had?"

"Just about." Summer nodded, then took a sip of her soda. "I've been running every test I could, and I think at this point I'm finally done. I'm just waiting for a few final results, but nothing is expected to be out of the ordinary on those."

"Has Jason contacted you?" Suzie smiled at the waitress as she delivered their plates of food. After she and Mary ordered their drinks, she turned her attention back to Summer. "About the mashed potatoes?"

"Yes, he did. That was a great help, Suzie. I was able to identify that the source of the poison was in one bowl, which put us all at ease that it's likely no one else ingested any poison." Summer shook her head. "I was very concerned that we might have quite a few cases of poisoning on our hands, but now I'm pretty much convinced that Jerome was targeted."

"Can you tell me a little bit more about the poison that was used?" Mary settled back in her chair and picked up one of her chicken fingers. She eyed it for a minute, then set it back down on her plate.

"The poison that was used, isn't a common household product." Summer took a bite of her chicken and closed her eyes as she savored it.

"So, it wouldn't be hanging around in a restaurant?" Suzie dipped a fry into some ketchup and popped it into her mouth.

"No. There's really no reason for it to be in the restaurant. In some cases, it is used in medications, but other than that it is primarily used for medical research. It is not harmful or lethal in small doses, but obviously in high doses it can be deadly.

Chemists like Ginger might use it in their lab to test out different reactions to it." Summer shrugged. "If someone had it in that kitchen, it was on purpose. This isn't something that can just be purchased. I would expect a scientist, or maybe a pharmacist to have access to it, but not your average person."

"Can't you get just about everything on the internet?" Mary nibbled a tiny bit of her chicken finger.

"There are some poisons that you could come across on the internet. But not this one. This one is highly regulated, and I just don't see how an average person would have access to it, unless it was given to them or someone they know for medical reasons." Summer frowned as she looked at Mary. "Aren't you hungry?"

"Yes, I am." Mary nodded. "All this talk of poison is making it hard for me to enjoy this. I've never thought about just how vulnerable food in a restaurant is. I mean, we have no idea who exactly is handling it, or what might be getting put in it."

"You can't let yourself fixate on that. Yes, it's true, we don't have much control over our food, even what we buy in the grocery store. But cases of intentional poisoning are extremely rare, and not something that you should be worried about in your everyday life." Summer took a big bite of her chicken finger. "See? Not worried."

"I guess I am being a little silly." Mary smiled.

"I don't think you're being silly at all." Suzie narrowed her eyes. "In fact, this reminds me of something."

"What's that?" Mary looked over at her.

"How Sam and Ginger have avoided eating just about everything at Dune House." Suzie pointed a fry at Mary. "They said they would get their meals elsewhere, remember?"

"Yes?" Mary shook her head. "Why is that important?"

"Because who would be more cautious about their food than someone who planned to poison someone else? It would make you paranoid, wouldn't it?" Suzie raised an eyebrow.

"That's a good point." Mary nodded slowly. "But they had no problem with going out to eat at Pelicans on the Pier."

"Maybe they went there in order to put poison in the food, but they didn't actually eat any food there. I mean, Ginger is the one suspect that we know of that probably had access to the hard-to-get poison that was used to kill Jerome." Suzie looked back at Summer. "I'd say that this case is pretty cut and dry."

"Unfortunately, suspicion isn't going to be enough." Summer leaned across the table and lowered her voice. "Without proof, some kind of evidence that connects them directly to the crime, it's not going to be enough to warrant an arrest. And, it shouldn't be." She looked between the two of them. "The chemical might be hard for most people to access, but that doesn't make it impossible. We can't just assume that because of Ginger's profession she had something to do with this. She might never have worked with it at all. I have no idea what she does in her workplace."

"That's true." Suzie signaled to the waitress. When she walked over, she smiled at her. "Can we have to-go boxes please?"

"Leaving already?" Summer picked up another chicken strip.

"Sorry Summer, but I think the best chance we have of finding out what Ginger was working with, is to spend some time with her, and Sam. Maybe we can find out something that will help."

"And they'll be leaving town by tomorrow more than likely." Mary narrowed her eyes. "We need to find out what we can, fast." She scraped her food into the to-go box she was handed. "Summer, thanks for the information."

"Sure, I think Jason is going to speak to them in more depth." Summer frowned. "If you do speak to them be careful. Don't push things too hard, or they might get the idea that you suspect them."

"We'll be careful." Mary nodded. On the way out the door she slipped the waitress the money to cover all of their meals, as well as a tip. "Make sure that she gets a piece of chocolate cake, too. She loves that." Mary winked at her, then followed Suzie out the door.

"That was sweet of you, Mary." Suzie flashed her a smile as they walked to the car. "Do you think Sam and Ginger will be at the house?"

"I'm not sure. But it's a good first place to check. Either way, I'm getting rid of anything that's open in the fridge." Mary frowned.

"Do you really think they might have put something in our food?" Suzie pulled open the door to the car and looked across the top of it at Mary.

"I'm not sure what to think. But I'm not going to take any chances." Mary met Suzie's eyes. "I think we need to be cautious, extremely cautious, especially if we're going to continue looking into this. Summer is right, if the killer suspects that we have figured something out, then we might become targets, too." She shuddered at the thought.

"You're right. From now on, we only eat what we make, from our own kitchen." Suzie frowned.

As they drove back towards Dune House, Mary's heart pounded. She hated the thought of suspecting Ginger and Sam, but at the moment she didn't see any other options.

CHAPTER 10

*S*uzie felt some relief as she pulled into the parking lot of Dune House and spotted Sam and Ginger's rental car parked there.

"It looks like they're home." She parked beside their car.

"And alone in the house." Mary looked over at her with a tight frown. "Who knows what they might be doing."

"Let's try not to get too paranoid, Mary." Suzie met her eyes. "We don't know if they were involved in anything yet."

"And we don't know if they weren't." Mary stepped out of the car.

Suzie frowned as she watched Mary walk ahead

of her. She hated to see Mary worried. But she couldn't blame her for being concerned.

When they stepped inside, Ginger and Sam were just past the foyer, in the dining room.

"Hi there." Suzie smiled at them both. "I'm glad we caught you. I just wanted to make sure that you have everything that you need."

"Yes, I think we're just fine." Ginger nodded to her and smiled in return. "We went on a nice, long hike this morning."

"Long, very long." Sam reached down and rubbed the fronts of his thighs. "I don't think I'm built for the outdoor life."

"You did good once we got started." Ginger winked at him.

"I'm going to lay down for a bit." Sam glanced between Suzie and Mary, then looked at the stairs in the kitchen. "It's been a busy morning."

"Oh Sam, I wanted to go to the beach." Ginger frowned as she caught his hand.

"Ginger, I can't." He sighed as he looked at her. "I know that you want to get every last minute of activity out of this vacation, but I need to rest. You know that I didn't get much sleep last night."

"I know." Ginger released his hand and nodded. "You're right. Go on, I'll be up in a minute."

"Or, if you'd like, we could all go for a stroll on the beach." Suzie smiled at Ginger. "I'm sure Pilot would enjoy a chance to get a good run in."

"Really?" Ginger's lips quirked up into a smile. "I'd love that, a girls' trip to the beach."

"Yes." Mary grinned. "I'll pack us some drinks so that way we can enjoy the sunny afternoon. If we have a few more days like this, the water will start to warm up. Too bad you two can't stay a little longer."

"I have been trying to talk Sam into staying a bit longer." Ginger slid her hands back through her hair. "We could really use the break. But he's too logical to agree."

"I bet you could use a break." Suzie grabbed the soft-sided cooler from Mary that she had stocked with bottles of water and ice packs and slung it over her shoulder. "I imagine your work can be very demanding."

"Demanding isn't the right word." Ginger shook her head as she followed them to the door. "I don't think there's been a word invented in the English language that could describe the pressure I am under most days."

"That sounds awful." Mary opened the door, and Pilot bolted past her, straight for the sand.

"It is rough sometimes. I get a lot of pressure to produce results that certain companies want, but that's not always what happens, and then I have to endure their reactions. I think I get yelled at more than someone working in retail." Ginger descended the steps to the trail that led to the beach.

"I'm glad you're getting a little break then." Suzie matched her pace. "I wish it could be longer."

"Me, too." Ginger laughed as Pilot bounded after a seagull.

"Couldn't you just decide to stay?" Mary glanced over at her. "Or does Sam make those decisions?"

"Oh no, it's nothing like that." Ginger grinned. "Trust me, I'm usually the one making the final call. But in this case, he's right. We've been having some financial trouble, and we have a plan to get things straightened out. The more we stray from the plan, the less likely it's going to happen. So, he does remind me of that and try to keep me on track. But his job isn't as pressured as mine. I guess he can't understand why I'd rather be out playing in the sun, instead of back home working to pay off our debt." She cleared her throat. "Don't get me wrong, we have enough money, but we were both hoping to retire early and do some traveling, so we're trying to tighten our budget like crazy. I had to convince him to come on this trip."

"I bet you needed it." Mary shook her head. "It sounds like any time away from your work would be helpful."

"I did need it. I love what I do. I love getting to explore chemicals, and potentially come across breakthroughs. But it is never going to be relaxing. Actually, the only reason we were able to come is because there was a spill at the lab, and it closed for the week." Ginger picked up a piece of driftwood and tossed it across the sand for Pilot to fetch.

"That sounds scary." Suzie squinted against the sunlight as she looked at her. "What happened?"

"I'm not sure exactly. Someone on the janitorial staff apparently got into something they shouldn't have and spilled some chemicals all over the floor. Of course, he claims that it wasn't him, that he just found it like that, but he can't prove it. He says that there were signs that someone broke in. Anyway, my boss is investigating it and no matter what happened it was unpredictable how the chemicals would react together, so they brought in a special cleaning crew and wanted to give the lab time to air out before anyone is allowed back in."

"Aren't there cameras in the lab, to show if the

janitor did it?" Mary tugged the stick free from Pilot's mouth and tossed it again for him.

"Not inside the lab. There are some outside the lab, but they're not always working. The company that owns the lab insists on no cameras inside because some of the work we do is classified. It's too much of a risk to have any of our activity recorded." Ginger laughed as Pilot splashed into the water and snapped at a wave that rushed towards him.

"Wow, it sounds like you might as well be in a spy movie." Mary kicked a bit of sand into the air. "It might be stressful, but I'm sure it's very important work."

"I like to think so." Ginger paused and turned to look out over the water. "But then I see beauty like this, and I think about how many hours a day I'm stuck inside, peering through microscopes, sifting through deadly chemicals, and I wonder what is really more important." She took a deep breath of the salty air. "You two were smart. You combined your work with living in such an amazing place."

"Maybe." Suzie stepped up to the water beside her. "But running a bed and breakfast isn't going to save lives. Medications can help save lives. You're responsible for developing medications, aren't you?"

"Yes. That's true." A faint smile passed across

Ginger's lips. "It does feel good when I hear that I've been involved in developing a treatment for something serious. I had a part in creating heart medication for a condition that strikes mostly women, in their early forties. Many times, they don't even think about having heart issues, and by the time they're diagnosed it's too late. But with this medication, they're getting a longer life." She took another deep breath. "Thank you for reminding me of that. It does make the pressure worth it when I feel like I'm making a difference."

"You do make a difference." Suzie smiled. "But that doesn't mean you don't deserve a vacation. There's some beach chairs set up ahead. Why not soak up some sun for a little while?"

"That sounds perfect." Ginger nodded, then headed up the beach towards the chairs.

Mary stepped closer to Suzie. "Interesting, hmm?"

"Very." Suzie crossed her arms as she watched Ginger grow smaller. By all accounts she seemed sweet and harmless, still, a shiver crept up along Suzie's spine.

hile Ginger was on the beach, and Sam was upstairs resting, Mary took the time to clean out the refrigerator. Although she did think she was being a little paranoid, she knew she wouldn't be able to rest until she was sure that there was nothing that could put any of them at risk. She even tossed out Pilot's dog food and washed both of his bowls, just in case. By the time she was done, she was a little worn out.

Mary stepped out onto the deck just in time to see Ginger walking back towards the house. She watched the woman approach and tried to imagine her putting poison in Jerome's food. It was unlikely that she had access to the kitchen, so she would have had to put it in at the table. Wouldn't someone else have noticed that? Someone who sat close to them, or someone that served the food? She knew that Sean had made no mention of seeing anything suspicious. But he had also told Suzie that it was very busy, and he was feeling overwhelmed. Maybe the chaos in the restaurant was enough to cover up someone slipping a bit of poison into someone's mashed potatoes. She waved to Ginger, but the woman didn't wave back. Something else had her attention.

Mary looked in the direction that she did and saw a police officer and a man in a suit walking towards Ginger. Mary clenched her teeth. She knew that Suzie had sent Jason a text letting him know that Sam and Ginger were at the house. It was only a matter of time before someone was sent over to question them. However, these men didn't lead Ginger towards the house. Instead they remained a few feet away from the porch with her.

Ginger took a step back and shook her head.

Mary couldn't hear what she said at first, then Ginger's voice grew louder.

"That is ridiculous. How could you even ask me that?"

Mary's muscles tensed. She could feel the tension between Ginger and the man in the suit rising. She decided to get a little closer, just in case things got out of hand.

"Ma'am, I just need to ask you a few more questions." The man spoke in a calm, but stern voice.

"You can't. You can't ask me questions like that. How horrifying. I was there last night. Obviously, you know that. I saw what happened to that poor man. To think that you would even consider that I would do something like that is highly offensive." Ginger's voice wavered, followed by a faint gasp.

"It's important that we find out everything we can about what happened last night." The man softened his tone.

As Mary neared the pair, she recognized the man. It was Detective Kirk Rondella, Jason's partner.

"I've been trying to forget about it all day." Ginger wiped at her eyes as she took a shaky breath. "My poor husband couldn't sleep at all. He kept thinking that his stomach was upset, he had a headache. I thought I was going to have to take him to the hospital because he was so scared that he ate something that had been poisoned." She frowned. "That's not bad enough? Now you're asking me if I did it?"

"That's not what I'm asking, ma'am." Kirk

shifted his feet. He glanced briefly at Mary, then looked back at Ginger. "I'm asking if you have ever worked with the particular substance that was used to commit this crime."

"I can't answer that. I won't." Ginger took a big step back and held up her hands. "I know my rights. You can't force me to incriminate myself."

"I'm not trying to force you to do anything." Kirk's eyes remained on her. "However, it does always look better if you're willing to cooperate with an investigation."

"I won't be intimidated." Ginger caught sight of Mary. "Can you believe this? Did you hear what he asked me?"

"I'm sorry, Ginger, I'm not sure what's going on." Mary stepped closer to her. Her eyes darted from Ginger, to Kirk, and back again. "But I do know that Detective Rondella is just trying to do his job. I'm sure it's not easy for him to ask these questions."

"His job is not to accuse me of murder." Ginger crossed her arms. "His job is to find out who actually killed this man. Now, are you going to arrest me, or can I go?" She looked back at Kirk.

"I'm not here to arrest you, ma'am. But if you'd be willing to answer a few more questions for me, I would greatly appreciate it." Kirk held up one hand. "I'm just looking for information here. You may have more knowledge about this particular drug than anyone else right now. To be honest, we could use your help."

"My help?" Ginger narrowed her eyes. Her voice sharpened as she spoke. "How stupid do you think I am? If I give you any of my expert help, it will just make me look more guilty, and you won't call me cooperative when you put the cuffs on my wrists, will you?"

"Again, I'm not here to arrest you." Kirk frowned. "Here's my card." He held out a business card to her. "If you change your mind, and would like to share any information with me, please contact me."

"Sure, I'll do that." Ginger pursed her lips as she snatched the card from his hand.

"Mary." Kirk nodded to her, then turned and walked back towards the parking lot.

"This is insane. Absolutely insane." Ginger scowled at Kirk's back. Then she took a sharp breath and turned to look at Mary. "This is because of you, isn't it?" She stared hard at her. "After what we talked about earlier, you called the police and told them, didn't you?"

"No Ginger, I didn't." Mary caught her hand and gave it a light rub. "I understand why you're upset, but the police are going to question everyone who was there that night. Everyone who might have seen something, might know something. It's the only way they're going to find the killer. I know it's hard to be questioned like that, but please try not to take it personally."

"This is all just too much." Ginger pulled her hand away, then walked past Mary, into the house.

Mary watched as Ginger slid the door shut behind her. It was clear that Ginger was shaken up by Kirk's visit. But why? Was it because she was offended that she was questioned, or was it because she was surprised that they figured it out so fast?

With her heart still pounding, Mary walked back into the house as well. As she stepped in, she found Suzie in the dining room, staring at the stairs that led to the second floor.

Mary slid the door shut, as Suzie turned to look at her.

"What's with Ginger? She just blew past me and ignored me when I tried to ask her what was wrong." Suzie frowned. "Did something happen? Are you okay?"

"Kirk just questioned her about the murder."

Mary spoke in a hushed voice, afraid that Ginger might be listening in. She grabbed Suzie's hand and pulled her close. Then she whispered in her ear. "I think we need to talk to the chef, no matter what it takes. We need to figure out what happened, before all of this spins out of control."

Suzie nodded in agreement. She pulled out her phone, and dialed Jason's number. As she did, she started towards the front door.

Mary followed after her.

"Jason? Mary and I are coming down to the station. We were hoping to get a few minutes with the suspect you have in custody. Cody."

"Suzie, I don't think that's such a good idea."

"We'll talk about it when I get there." Suzie gestured for Mary to follow her. As they reached the car, Jason sighed in her ear.

"Fine, I'll be here."

"He sounds tired," Suzie muttered as she ended the call. "He definitely needs some help."

"You don't think it's bothering him that we're just going to show up and ask to talk to Cody?" Mary settled in the passenger seat.

"Maybe, but once he understands why, he'll be fine with it." Suzie put the car in drive and headed for the police station. After she parked, she walked into the station with Mary at her side.

"Are you sure about this?" Mary stepped through the door behind Suzie. "I don't want to upset Jason."

"Trust me, he's already upset, and he will continue to be upset until he puts the killer behind bars." Suzie smiled at the officer at the desk, then walked past it into the hallway that she knew would lead to Jason's office.

"I'm going to see if I can find Kirk." Mary walked off down another hallway.

Suzie nodded to her, but continued on to Jason's office, full of determination.

"Suzie." Jason greeted her at the door and gestured for her to come inside. "Why exactly do you think you need to talk to Cody?"

"It couldn't hurt, could it? He knows me, he might be more forthcoming with information with me." Suzie looked into Jason's eyes. "I know that you have already questioned him, and I'm sure that you and your officers have questioned him several times. Have you been able to make any progress?"

"No." Jason wiped his hand across his face, his fingers splayed over the stubble that had begun to grow on his cheeks. "In fact, we are going to release him soon if we don't come up with something substantial to keep him in custody. Just him being in the kitchen at the time of the murder is not enough to keep him behind bars."

"Maybe he'd say something to me." As Jason lowered his hand, Suzie met his eyes. "It might throw him off to have someone who isn't a police officer, someone who he knows, talk to him. I won't question him, just act like a friend, see what I can find out."

"It's certainly an unusual thing to do." Jason frowned, as he looked at her. "But you're right, it couldn't hurt. Worst case scenario, he may say nothing at all."

"Great. Then let me talk to him." Suzie rubbed her hands together. "I will give it my best shot. Maybe he will slip up and say something that you can use to prove his involvement."

"I hope so." Jason rubbed his hand over his head. "Things didn't go well when Kirk tried to question Ginger."

"I'll do my best to convince her to be more cooperative." Suzie walked beside him as he led her to one of the interrogation rooms.

"We've already been questioning Cody this morning, so he's inside. Here are the ground rules."

Jason turned to face her, his expression stern. "No inciting him, understand? I don't want to hear shouting of any kind. You are not a trained interrogator. You're not in there to get a confession. If he happens to say something that is useful, that's great, but it's not your job to get him to do that."

"I understand." Suzie locked her eyes to his.

"I'll be beside you the whole time." Jason started to open the door.

"Jason, wait." Suzie placed her hand over his. "Don't you think it would be a little more surprising if I just walked in there on my own? If he sees me with you, he might just go silent. But if I walk in on my own, he's going to be more relaxed. He will probably be more forthcoming with information."

"Suzie, I don't like that idea." Jason frowned.

"I'll be careful, I promise." Suzie held his gaze. "You know I'm right, Jason."

"I'll be watching." Jason pushed the door open, but remained outside in the hall, as she stepped in.

CHAPTER 12

The click of the door closing behind Suzie made her muscles tense up. She had asked to be alone with Cody, but now that she was actually alone with him, she wondered if that was wise. His large frame huddled in a small chair. His folded arms on the table looked massive as they stretched against the t-shirt he wore.

"Who are you?" Cody lifted his head from his arms. "What are you doing here?"

"I'm Suzie, remember?" Suzie smiled. "I own Dune House."

"That's right." Cody cleared his throat. "Nice place."

"I just wanted to see how you are going." Suzie shrugged.

"Great, I'm behind bars for something I didn't do." Cody scowled.

"Maybe I can help you with that." Suzie sat down across from him and tried not to show the fact that her legs trembled a bit. "I thought maybe we could talk about what happened last night."

"How are you going to help me?"

"Before my new life as an owner of a bed and breakfast, I used to do some investigative reporting." Suzie shrugged. "This crime, it's drawn my attention. Mostly because the police were so quick to arrest you. I wanted to see why that is and help you if possible."

"You noticed that, huh?" Cody frowned. "One minute I'm doing my job, the next I'm behind bars. Where's the justice in that?"

"That's what I'm wondering. Have they been treating you okay?" Suzie studied his face.

"So far." Cody straightened up in his chair. "They just keep asking me the same questions over and over again."

"That must be frustrating." Suzie sighed. "Have you had a chance to speak to your lawyer?"

"This morning." Cody nodded. "He says as long as I stay quiet and don't give them a reason to keep me, they have to release me."

"That's good, at least." Suzie frowned. "I'm sorry they were so quick to accuse you. Why do you think they did that?"

"I'm a criminal." Cody shook his head. "Once you have a rap sheet, you're always going to be the first one they slap the cuffs on."

"So, you don't think it has anything to do with the fact that you were the one that was in the kitchen when this happened?" Suzie's heart skipped a beat as she wondered if he would sense her shift in questioning.

"Yeah, I was in the kitchen when it happened. Of course, I was. I'm the chef. So was the dish-washer, so was the sous chef, so were many members of the waitstaff. It's ridiculous that I'm the only one behind bars." Cody balled his hands into fists.

"You're right." Suzie did her best to keep her voice steady, though the flex of his knuckles made her scoot back a little in her chair. "Did you know the man that died?"

"No, I didn't know him." Cody glared at her. "Why are you really asking me all of these ques-tions? You're acting like you're on my side, but you're asking me the same questions the cops did."

"There's no need to get upset, Cody. I'm just

trying to figure out exactly what happened here. Did you notice anyone else in the kitchen, acting a little suspiciously? Maybe someone sneaking around?" Suzie met his eyes and hoped her voice was soothing enough to settle him down.

"Get out." Cody scowled at her. "I don't want to say another word to you. You think I don't know what you're doing? What is this, some kind of strange good cop bad cop routine? I've done this dance before, lady, and I'm not interested. I'm not saying another word until I get released." He crossed his arms and tightened his lips.

Suzie sighed as she stood up from the table. "Suit yourself, Cody, but the only way you're going to be able to move on from this, is if the police are able to find the real killer. You might want to think about helping them out with that."

He stared hard at the table and didn't say a single word.

Suzie knocked lightly on the door. She glanced back at Cody, whose cheeks had reddened with anger. When the door swung open, she stepped out into the hall.

Jason closed the door behind her.

"I'm sorry, Jason. I think I might have made things worse."

"Don't be." Jason shook his head and leaned against the door. "He said more to you than he has to anyone else. Unfortunately, it's nothing that can help the investigation. He'll be free to go in about an hour. I'm not sure that I'll ever be able to get him to talk. But at least if he's out, I can track him, see if he talks to anyone else that works at the restaurant."

"That's something." Suzie nodded as she walked beside him towards the front of the station.

"It's really not." Jason spread his hands out in front of him. "But it's all I've got."

$\sim$

Mary met Suzie at the front of the station. She gave Jason a short wave as he walked away.

"I couldn't find Kirk, I guess he's still out working the case." Mary slipped her hands into her pockets. "Did you have any luck with Cody?"

"I'll tell you about it on the drive home." Suzie led her back out to the parking lot. In the few minutes it took to get back to Dune House she managed to recount her entire conversation with Cody. "So, you see, I got absolutely nothing from him. I know Jason is just as frustrated as I am. And tired."

Pilot greeted them at the door.

"I'll make us some coffee." Mary hurried to the kitchen and Pilot went to his empty dish. He stood in front of it eagerly.

"Hungry pal, let me get you some food." As the dog food clanged into the metal bowl, Mary's own stomach twisted with hunger. While the coffee brewed, she threw together a platter of cheese and crackers for her and Suzie to share.

"Oh, Mary that coffee smells delicious." Suzie walked into the kitchen and sniffed the air.

"Perfect timing. You grab the coffee, and I'll bring the food. Let's eat outside so we'll have a little privacy, just in case Sam and Ginger show up." Mary poured coffee into two cups.

"If they haven't taken off yet." Suzie cringed.

"After the way that Ginger reacted to Kirk's questioning, I'd be surprised if they didn't." Mary followed Suzie out onto the porch and set the coffee down on the table beside the tray of food.

"So, do you think he did it?" Mary blew some steam from her cup of coffee. "I mean, what does your gut instinct tell you?"

"I'm just not sure." Suzie sighed as she glanced out over the water. "I won't say I wasn't nervous being around him, but I know that he has a history of violence, so that is to be expected. It doesn't mean that he's guilty of this particular crime." She looked back at Mary. "I have to say that he didn't act guilty. He didn't try to tell a bunch of lies about why he couldn't have done it. He didn't accuse anyone else in particular. But then he knew he was due to be released, so he might not have felt the need to deflect suspicion." She picked up her cup of coffee. "All I know for sure is that Cody definitely had access to the food. However, I can't put the poison in his possession. Jason hasn't been able to find a connection to the poison, either."

"Remember what Ginger said earlier?" Mary took a small sip of her coffee. "She said they'd been working on a heart medication at the lab. Didn't Summer mention something about the chemical that poisoned Jerome being used in some medications?"

"Yes, she did." Suzie narrowed her eyes. "What are you thinking, Mary?"

"Well, maybe that's how Cody got the poison. Maybe, he is taking that medication for some reason." Mary tapped her fingertip against the table.

"Maybe he crushed it up and dumped it in the potatoes."

"Maybe, but Ginger said the medication she was working on was targeted to treat women. One thing Cody is not, is a woman." Suzie took a drink from her coffee cup, then set it down. "However, maybe he has access to the medication. Maybe he knows someone that uses it."

"That's possible." Mary nodded. "Does he have a girlfriend?"

"I'm not sure. But if he does, I imagine he's going to have to replace the medicine he used, or the person it belongs to is going to notice it's missing. Of course, it is possible that the same chemical is used in other medication. Cody gets released soon. I say we stake out the pharmacies." Suzie pulled out her phone. "There's only one in Garber and a bigger one in Parish, near the border. I'll bet that when he gets released, he'll want to replace that medicine fast, so that the cops don't make the connection."

"That is if there is even a connection." Mary stood up from the table. "I think this is a good way to find out. You take one pharmacy, and I'll take the other."

"Good plan." Suzie caught her by the hand and

pulled her gently back down into her chair. "After we eat."

"Better plan." Mary grinned, then took a bite of a cracker.

After they finished their food, the two split off in different directions.

CHAPTER 13

ary drove her SUV towards the pharmacy at the edge of Parish. After double-checking the information she had about Cody, she saw that his address was nearby. If he did have a girlfriend who needed medication, it was likely that this was the pharmacy she would use. She parked and walked inside. She waved hello to Mick, the pharmacist, then walked down one of the aisles.

As Mary pretended to browse through different bottles of vitamins, she kept an eye on the pharmacy. It wasn't very busy. One teenage boy, one older gentleman, and a woman who appeared to be in her sixties, each took a turn at the pick-up window. No one that she thought might be in a relationship with Cody. As she continued to watch, her cell phone rang. Wes' name flashed across the screen.

"Hi Wes." Mary smiled. It seemed to be a habit when she said his name, to smile.

"Mary, I just went by Dune House to see you, but no one was there. Where are you?"

"I'm at a pharmacy." Mary turned away from the pick-up window and lowered her voice. "I'm on a stakeout."

"A what? Where are you? Which pharmacy?" Wes sighed.

"Don't worry, it's nothing serious. Suzie had a theory and we are trying to see if it will play out. But this place is so quiet, I doubt that I'm going to spot the person we are looking for. What are you up to?" Mary glanced over at the pick-up window just in time to see the pharmacist flip the sign on the window to closed. "Oh, and it just closed."

"Perfect. Where can I meet you?"

"I'm on the other side of town. I can meet you at Dune House if you want." Mary smiled at the thought of seeing him.

"Sounds good, I'll wait for you here. It looks like your guests just pulled in."

"Be there soon." Mary ended the call. As she left

the store, she noticed Travis walk up to the dispensing window. He stood beside the closed window for a moment, shook his head, then turned and walked the other way.

Mary trailed behind him as he walked through the store to the front register.

"Why is the prescription counter closed?" He rested his hands on the front counter and stared at the clerk.

"It closes at five today." The young woman stared at him.

"It's not five, yet. Not for five more minutes." Travis smacked one hand against the counter. "I needed to pick up some medication."

"I'm sorry, I can't do anything about that. Would you like the number to our corporate office?" She picked up a pen.

"No thank you." Travis scowled at her. "But you can tell them, they just lost a customer."

As Travis stalked out of the pharmacy, Mary wondered what kind of medication he was picking up. As far as she knew he wasn't in the restaurant at the time of Jerome's death, but that didn't mean that he couldn't have paid someone to do his dirty work.

∾

*S*uzie glanced at her watch. If Jason's prediction was right, then Cody had been a free man for about an hour. He certainly hadn't hit the pharmacy right away. Nor had she seen any women approach the pharmacy to pick up medication. She began to search on her phone for any information about Cody and a potential girlfriend. As she tried to narrow down his social profiles, she heard a familiar voice.

"Picking up for Mildred Spenna."

Suzie looked up to see Sean at the pick-up window.

Suzie watched as the pharmacist handed him a white paper bag. From previous research she knew that Mildred was his mother.

As Suzie watched him walk away her heart pounded harder. She didn't want to think it, and she didn't want to believe it. But she couldn't avoid it.

"You're probably jumping to conclusions, Suzie," she muttered to herself as she shook her head and left the pharmacy.

A quick glance at her watch told her she might make it to the medical examiner's office in time to catch Summer. On the drive there she listed reasons why Sean couldn't possibly be the killer. He was too young to do something like that. He was barely an adult. Why would he want to murder someone? Of course, that was a ridiculous reason not to be a killer. He had no history with Jerome that she knew of, no motive. Of course, that didn't mean that he didn't do it. Could she have missed the fact that he was a murderer? She slammed on her brakes as she reached the medical examiner's office, then jumped out of the car. She'd just pushed the car door shut behind her when she spotted Summer on her way out the door.

"Summer." Suzie waved to her as she ran up to her.

"Suzie, is everything okay?" Summer frowned. "You look stressed."

"I am stressed. A little. Summer, you said that the poison can be used in some medications. What kind of medications would they be?" Suzie tried to catch her breath.

"Heart medications mostly." Summer narrowed her eyes. "Why?"

"Could the medicine be used to poison someone, instead of just the chemical itself?" Suzie raised an eyebrow. "I mean, would it have come up the same way in the tests you did?"

"I would say so, yes in high doses. But it's not a

common medication. It's used for specific heart conditions. According to Jason none of his suspects are on the medication." Summer shifted her purse on her shoulder and began to walk towards her car. "Why? Did you find something?"

Suzie's heart pounded against her chest. She couldn't be certain that Sean's mother was on the specific medication that Summer mentioned, but she knew that it was a possible link. She'd grown to like Sean, and the last thing she wanted to do was get him into trouble. But what if he was the killer? What if he had taken some of his mother's medication, and that was why he picked up a new prescription for her? She had to be sure before she sent Jason straight to Sean's front door.

"Thanks for the information, Summer." Suzie turned and hurried back to her car.

"Suzie?" Summer called after her.

Suzie climbed into her car and left the parking lot before Summer could catch up to her. As she drove in the direction of Sean's house, she wondered how she would find out the truth. It wasn't as if he would just volunteer the information. He wouldn't spontaneously confess to being a killer. But she still felt as if being able to be face to face with him would tell her something. As she stepped onto the porch, she took a deep breath, and focused on trying not to tip him off about what she knew. Her knuckles struck the hard wood twice before the door swung open. Sean peered out at her his brows knitted.

"Hi Sean." Suzie offered him a warm smile. "I just wanted to see how you and your mom are doing with everything that's happened."

"I'm okay, I guess. My mom's okay so far. I've been keeping the television off so she can't see the news. But I'm not sure how long that will last." Sean opened the door farther for her. "You can come inside."

"Thanks." Suzie stepped in and looked around the living room in search of his mother. The furniture was sparse and older, but in good shape.

"She's in her room, resting. But we need to keep our voices down." Sean glanced down a short hallway.

"Sean. Did you get my pills?" A frail voice called out from a room down the hall.

"Oh yeah, Mom, I did." Sean grabbed the paper bag from the side table and hurried towards the bedroom.

Suzie followed him but paused at a respectful distance as he stepped inside.

"Did you tell the police what happened? Are

they going to do anything about it?" Mildred's voice shook with each word she spoke.

"No Mom, I told you. They won't do anything about it. I'm just glad the doctor let us get a new prescription. I have a guest, Mom, I'll bring you some juice in just a minute." Sean stepped back out of her room and turned back to face Suzie. "Sorry about that, she gets a little anxious about her medicine."

"I understand, it's important to her." Suzie looked up at him as he passed her to step back into the living room. "What did she mean about telling the police? What happened?"

"Oh." Sean shoved his hands into his pockets. "When I picked up her last prescription, I got mugged on the way home from the pharmacy. Luckily, the doctor was willing to give her a new prescription."

"Mugged?" Suzie's eyes widened. "Here in Garber?"

"Yeah, I was down by the docks because I needed to pick up something from one of the boats I've been working on, and it was dark. The guy came out of nowhere. Knocked me out, took the pharmacy bag. I guess he must have thought I had something that he could use to get high." Sean shook his head. "My mom was upset, but you know the police aren't going to be able to do anything about it."

"You could at least make a report, give them a description of the man." Suzie watched as he sat down on the couch.

"I didn't see him. At all. He sucker-punched me and knocked me down. Next thing I knew, he was running off with the medication. I was more concerned about getting her a new prescription than I was with him." Sean shrugged. "With no description the cops would never catch him. There aren't any cameras in that area. Nothing I could have done. So, I decided to just focus on talking to her doctor and getting her a new prescription. I'm just really glad he did one." He frowned. "Sorry, she isn't up for visitors. I appreciate you coming by, though."

"You have so much to handle." Suzie swept her gaze around the living room, which she guessed was kept tidy by Sean. "Do you ever have any help with your mom?"

"Not really." Sean looked towards the front window that overlooked the porch. "Sometimes the neighbors will come by just to visit her. She likes that. But she can't talk for too long, it takes a lot out of her."

"Maybe you could let me know when she's feeling up to it, and I could come by to visit. I'd love to tell her what a great job you did when you worked with Paul. I didn't realize you were working with another fisherman." Suzie perched on the edge of the couch and watched his expression. Could he be lying about everything?

"Yeah, I do now and then, when I have time. I'm basically just trying to learn as much as I can. If I ever have enough money to get my own boat, I think I would like to make a living that way. The thing is, I can't be away from my mother for long trips. So, it's really just a dream of mine right now." Sean met her eyes. "Have you heard any updates on the investigation? Do they know who killed that guy, yet?"

"Not yet. In fact, Cody has been released." Suzie stood up from the couch. "They weren't able to prove that he put the poison in the potatoes."

"If not him, then who?" Sean sat back against the couch and closed his eyes. "I hope they figure it out soon. Keeping this from my mom hasn't been easy."

"I'm sure it hasn't." Suzie edged towards the door. "Thanks for your time, Sean."

"Sure, no problem." Sean smiled at her as she opened the door. "I'll let you know when my mom is up for a visit."

"Good." Suzie smiled at him in return, then stepped out onto the porch. Her chest tightened as she realized what she had to do. Sean had a lot of responsibility on his shoulders, but his story didn't make sense. Why wouldn't he report a mugging? She guessed that he had lied about losing the medication, so that he could get his mother a new bottle. Which meant he had an entire bottle of medication that might contain the same substance that poisoned Jerome.

Suzie glanced back over her shoulder and through the front window, into the house. She caught sight of Sean carrying a glass of juice to his mother's bedroom. What would happen to her if Jason decided to arrest Sean?

Suzie pushed the thought from her mind as she walked back to her car. As she opened the driver's side door, her cell phone rang. Mary's name flashed across the screen. She brushed her finger across the answer option and put the phone to her ear.

"Mary? How is it going over there?"

"No sign of Cody, or anyone that might be dating him. At least, from what I can tell. Wes is at the house waiting for me."

"Great, I might need to pick his brain. See you there soon." Suzie took one last look in the direction of Sean's house, then started the car. As she drove back to Dune House, she tried to convince herself that turning Sean in was the right thing to do. However, by the time she parked, she still didn't think she could do it.

CHAPTER 14

Mary's eyes narrowed as she ended the call. A slight waver in Suzie's voice made her wonder if there was something that her friend wasn't telling her. She tucked her phone into her purse then headed back to Dune House. From Suzie's account, Travis' presence and behavior in the restaurant hung in her mind. He certainly did seem volatile. Had Jerome's interference in his life made such an impact that he wanted revenge enough to kill him? She pulled into the parking lot of Dune House. She spotted Wes on the porch. He leaned against the railing and waved to her.

Mary felt a faint flutter in her chest as she parked the SUV. Although she and Wes had been dating for some time, it still surprised her when she found him eager to see her. She walked up the steps and into his open arms.

"Hey there," Wes murmured in her ear as he embraced her. "It feels like it's been far too long since the last time I saw you."

"So much has happened." Mary frowned as she pulled away from him.

"Yes, I know it has. I'm sorry that you're in the middle of all of this." Wes looked into her eyes. "You're stressed, I can tell."

"I'm just worried." Mary shook her head as she crossed her arms. "It's unsettling to think that someone could be running around Garber poisoning people."

"It is." Wes nodded, then glanced towards the parking lot as a car pulled in. "It looks like Suzie is back."

"She has something she wants to ask you, I think." Mary turned to face the parking lot. "She sounded odd when I spoke to her on the phone."

"So did you." Wes wrapped his arm around her waist and pulled her closer to him. "What's Suzie got you up to?"

"It's always my fault, huh?" Suzie smiled as she joined them on the porch.

"Did I say that?" Wes' eyes widened as he smiled.

"You're not wrong." Suzie sighed as she perched on one of the rocking chairs beside the front door. "Are Sam and Ginger here?"

"I saw them pull in a little while ago." Wes gazed at Suzie. "Are you doing okay? You don't look so good."

"I'm okay." Suzie forced a smile. "Just trying to figure something out."

"Suzie, what's going on?" Mary sat down in the rocking chair beside her. Pilot greeted Suzie then went to Wes for a pat. "Do you have a new lead?"

"I'm not sure exactly. I guess, I'm hoping that I don't. But I can't deny that evidence is stacking up against him." Suzie closed her eyes.

"Against who? Cody?" Mary leaned forward to look at her.

"No, not Cody. Sean." Suzie looked up at Mary. "I don't want to believe it, but I think his mother is on the same medication that may have been used to poison Jerome. Also, he had to pick up a new prescription because he claimed the other one was stolen. It just seems like too much of a coincidence to me."

"That is some pretty important evidence." Wes

leaned against the railing in front of them. "Have you told Jason, yet?"

"No, I haven't." Suzie took a deep breath, then let it out slowly.

"Suzie." Mary met her eyes. "You know that you have to tell him."

"I know I do, but Sean is so young, and he takes care of his sick mother. There's no one else to help him. Besides, what could his motive possibly be to do this?" Suzie frowned. "There may be evidence there, a good reason to suspect him, but without a motive I don't think that means much."

"No offense intended, Suzie, but I don't really think that's for you to decide. Jason is the one with the experience, and the knowledge to decide who is a good suspect and who isn't." Wes frowned as he looked at her. "It's never easy to suspect someone who appears to be a good person on the surface, but Jerome deserves to have his murder solved."

"I know, I know." Suzie rubbed her hands across her face. "I am going to call him. I just wanted to take a minute to think things through. Why would Sean tell me about Jerome ordering a separate serve of mashed potatoes if he had put the poison in there?"

"Maybe, so he didn't look suspicious." Mary

suggested. "Maybe he had time to think about it after he spoke to the police and he knew he had to say something so he wouldn't look suspicious if it came out."

"Maybe. But I still don't believe he did this. I mean realistically we have another good suspect right here under our roof." She glanced towards the closed front door.

"Are you talking about Ginger?" Mary looked at the door as well, then turned back to Suzie. "Do you really think she did this?"

"Maybe? We don't know much about her or Sam." Suzie rocked slowly back and forth in the chair. "I just think that it's rather convenient that she's here, a chemist, at the same time that Jerome is poisoned with a chemical she probably had access to."

"I can't deny that." Mary slid her hands into the wide pockets in her skirt. "But why would she come all the way here to do it? She had to have known that Jerome would be here at the same time. And the same problem exists with her. What is the motive?"

"I'm not sure. But she did insist on coming here, her husband was not so eager." Suzie sighed, then lifted her eyes to Mary's. "And they were at the restaurant. Maybe there's some kind of connection between Jerome and Ginger that we don't know about."

"Maybe. I'll see what I can find out." Mary stood up. "She might open up to me. Wes, could we postpone our walk?" She met his eyes.

"Sure, we can. Let me know how it goes." Wes shifted his gaze to Suzie. "I guess you'll be going to see Jason?"

"I will be." Suzie nodded to him, then pulled out her phone.

Mary glanced back at the two of them briefly before she headed into the house. She spotted Ginger right away, perched on the couch in the living room with a cup of tea and a book.

"Here you are." Mary smiled as she stepped into the living room. "I was wondering where you two might have disappeared to. Is Sam resting comfortably?"

"For the moment. Poor fool didn't wear an ounce of sunscreen. I warned him." Ginger laughed and shook her head.

"You two are so sweet together." Mary watched as Ginger took a sip of her tea. "It's always inspiring to me when I see true romance."

"I have to admit, I didn't think it was ever going

to happen for me." Ginger swirled the tea in her cup. "I had pretty much given up after my first marriage ended in disaster. I thought I just wasn't destined to be in love."

"I know that feeling." Mary heard the distant sound of Wes' car pulling out of the parking lot. "My first marriage didn't go well, either."

"But you have a new romance, too, don't you?" Ginger glanced up at her with a warm glow in her eyes. "I saw you out there with that guy. Wes, right?"

"Oh Wes?" Mary shrugged and sat back. "He's certainly something I didn't expect."

"They always show up just when you think it's impossible." Ginger sighed. She lifted her cup of tea to her mouth and took a big swallow.

"Yes, I would agree with that. When things ended with my husband, I thought, that's it, Mary. You're alone for the rest of your life." She drew a deep breath.

"That must have been heartbreaking." Ginger placed her hand over Mary's.

"It actually wasn't." Mary smiled as her attention focused back on the woman across from her. "I'd been unhappy for a long time, and the idea of not having to pretend anymore, it gave me a sense of freedom. Sure, I was scared, but I was also relieved."

"I felt that way, too, to some degree. But also very guilty." Ginger tightened her grasp on the cup of tea.

"It's easy to feel guilty, but I'm sure it wasn't your fault. Sometimes we just don't meet the right person the first time, or the second, or the third." Mary smiled some. "No guarantees, right?"

"Yes, you're right. But I did have reason to feel guilty." Ginger took a sip of her tea. Her expression darkened. "I still do sometimes."

Sam walked into the dining room. "Ladies, where can I get some of that tea?"

"Let me get it for you." Mary stood up and hurried towards the kitchen. Ginger's words rolled through her mind. What did she carry guilt about?

CHAPTER 15

"*L*et's go, Pilot, you and me." Suzie called Pilot over to her side as she started down the front steps. She knew that Jason would be at the police station. He always worked late when he had a case. The first step would be to get to the station. Whether she could go through with telling Jason about Sean or not, she didn't know just yet. But she was sure that Jason could use a walk as much as she could. As she approached the police station, she sent Jason a text.

At the police station. Would you like to join Pilot and me for a walk?

Suzie slowed her strides as she expected that he might not respond for a few minutes, if at all. Instead, he responded almost immediately.

Sure, be right out.

Suzie tucked her phone into her pocket, then guided Pilot towards the front of the police station. She thought about the possibility that Sean could have committed the crime. Perhaps he had something against Jerome, or maybe he planned to kill someone else and put the poison in Jerome's food by accident. Whatever the reason he might have had, it was clear that he had the opportunity, and probably the poison to carry out the crime. Just because he seemed like a nice enough kid and had the sense of responsibility and care to look after his mother, that didn't make him innocent.

"Hey Suzie." Jason stepped out of the police station and crouched down to greet Pilot. "Hey buddy, good to see a friendly face." He ran his fingers through the dog's fur on the top of his head. Pilot's tail wagged eagerly.

"I bet you're exhausted." Suzie met his eyes as he stood back up.

"Running on adrenaline I think." Jason gestured to the sidewalk ahead of him. "Shall we?"

"Yes." Suzie began to walk beside him. She decided to wait just a little bit to reveal her suspicions. "How is the case going?"

"In too many directions at once." Jason frowned.

"Did you get the name of the man who was sitting right beside Jerome?" Suzie guided Pilot beside her as they continued down the sidewalk.

"I did. He left before Jerome died, but he was seated next to him." Jason glanced over at her. "It's Freddy Manchester."

"Freddy Manchester. That doesn't sound familiar to me." Suzie paused as Pilot investigated a patch of grass. "Do you know him?"

"No, he's not a local. I looked him up, but I couldn't find much about him. I'm still working on it." Jason squinted into the sky, then looked back at Suzie. "As for your guests. It has been confirmed that Ginger definitely had access to the substance that killed him, but I couldn't find a single bit of criminal history in either of their pasts."

"That doesn't surprise me." Suzie allowed Pilot to take the lead as they continued down the street. "They seem like good people. But they were both at the restaurant the night that Jerome was killed, and like you said Ginger had access to the substance that killed him." She paused again as Pilot found a lamp-post to sniff.

"That's true, and why they are still on my radar."

Jason winced. "So is Travis, but I can't get anything to stick to him. Plus, there is no evidence that he was at the restaurant that night. I am still waiting to get my hands on Jerome's computer, but I have his paper files. I have most of my officers combing through all of the files from Jerome's past clients and making calls and investigating leads, but they haven't come up with much."

"Do you have a picture of this Freddy?" Suzie glanced over at him. "Maybe I've seen him somewhere?"

"Maybe. He said he's been in town for about a week." Jason pulled out his phone, tapped the screen, then handed it to her. "That's him."

"Oh." Suzie's eyes widened as she saw the shock of blond hair. "I can't be certain, Jason, but this might be the same person that's been hanging around the docks. Paul had a bad feeling about him. You should send the picture to him, he can probably identify him for sure."

"Thanks, I'll do that." Jason took his phone back and typed out a text.

"If it is the same person, it makes me wonder, what is Freddy doing in town? He is alone, right? Paul says he's been hanging around the docks for a few days. He was asking the guys questions about the dock. He said it seemed a little strange."

"He claims that he's here to look into chartering a fishing boat." Jason reached down to stroke Pilot's fur. "He wants a break from the city life, but he's not ready to bite the bullet and buy a boat."

"It still seems odd to me that he would come out here to do that." Suzie narrowed her eyes as she looked farther down the street. A few people walked their dogs. Others sat on their porches. Everything was almost back to normal. But she knew the people of Garber wouldn't be content until the murder was solved.

"Maybe so. I checked into the records for boat sales and charters, there's actually been an uptick since last year. He claims a friend referred him to Garber. I haven't been able to get in touch with that friend, though." Jason matched Suzie's pace as she began to walk again. "I'm still digging into him. If you notice anything strange about Ginger and Sam, I'd like to hear about it. I couldn't get much out of them during their interview."

"I will see what I can find out." Suzie nodded. "How about the chef?" She tilted her head to the side so that she could meet his eyes.

"He's the main suspect at the moment. There's no way we can rule out the possibility that he put the poison in the mashed potatoes. But at this point we also have no way to prove that he did. The fact that he was there, and he had the opportunity makes him more likely to be our culprit. But I haven't been able to find any connection between him and Jerome, so that leaves me with no motive. Then there's Travis, who has plenty of motive, but I can't find anyone who puts him anywhere near the restaurant that day. He also doesn't have an alibi. He claims he was alone at home. I can't rule him in, and I can't rule him out." He held out his hands in front of him. "A lot of ideas, but not much evidence to go on."

"Well, I may have a little more to add." Suzie gritted her teeth as she turned to face him.

"What do you mean?" Jason met her eyes.

"Sean, the waiter from the restaurant. I don't believe that he was involved, but there is evidence to support the possibility." As Suzie filled him in on what she had observed, he pulled out his notebook to write down the information.

"I'll get on this right away."

"Jason, please, just make sure you have something solid before you think of making an arrest. Sean is a good kid from what I can tell, and his mother depends on him to take care of her." Suzie looked into his eyes. "I know you can't bend the rules, but please consider all options before you take that step."

"You're right, Suzie, I can't bend the rules. I appreciate you coming to me with this information, even if you don't believe he is the killer. I will look into it, and I can promise you that I will follow all of the steps I need to before I make an arrest. Okay?" Jason gazed back at her. "You can trust me on this."

"Thank you, Jason." Suzie patted Pilot's head. "Let's go home, buddy."

Pilot changed direction and ran towards Dune House, eager to go back.

CHAPTER 16

*M*ary stood on the porch and watched as Suzie and Pilot approached. She could tell from the slump of Suzie's shoulders that she had a lot on her mind.

"Hey Suzie." Mary climbed down the front steps to greet her at the end of the walkway. "Had a nice walk, Pilot?" She scratched behind his ear.

"We had a talk with Jason." Suzie looked up at her with a frown. "I told him about Sean."

"That's good, Suzie, I know it feels awful, but I'm sure it was the right thing to do. I actually think there's more we need to find out about Ginger. Our conversation left me thinking she might be hiding something." Mary straightened up and glanced back at the house. "I think we need to look into her previous marriage."

"Do you think it will lead to something?" Suzie raised an eyebrow.

"I think it might." Mary shrugged. "I could be wrong, though."

"I think we need to find out more about Travis." Suzie set Pilot free from his leash. "Jason can't find any evidence that he was anywhere near the restaurant. But it occurred to me that perhaps he paid someone else to be there. Maybe, he didn't need to be there to commit the crime."

"Someone else? Like the chef?" Mary met her eyes.

"Or the waiter." Suzie crossed her arms. "Sean certainly doesn't have a steady income. Maybe Travis figured out that Sean's mother was on a medicine that could be used as poison and offered Sean a deal that he couldn't refuse. It's a bit of a stretch, but I do think it's a possibility."

"You're right, it is possible." Mary pursed her lips, then shook her head. "But we'd have to be able to prove a connection between Travis and Sean."

"It's the last thing I want to do. But if there is a connection there, I want to find it before Jason does. I don't want it to be a surprise." Suzie started up the steps towards the house. "Do you want to see what you can find out about Ginger's past? I'm going to try to set up a meeting with Travis in the morning. Then I'm going to see what I can find out about this man that has popped up in town. Freddy. He was at the restaurant and seated right next to Jerome. Jason can find no connection between him and Jerome, but it might take a little more digging to get to it."

"Sure, I'll handle Ginger. Let me know what you come up with about Freddy." Mary followed her into the house. "Make sure you eat something too, Suzie."

"I will, if you will." Suzie winked at her.

After she made both herself and Suzie a sandwich, Mary headed to her room. She wasn't sure what she could find out about Ginger, but she knew she had to find it fast. Suzie had taught her a lot about searching for information about people. Ginger and Sam would be checking out the next day, and even if Jason tried to convince them to stay, they wouldn't have to. If there was some kind of connection between them and Jerome's death, it had to be found, quickly. She settled in with her computer and began to search Ginger's name. She managed to find her maiden name and began a search with that. Finding some information linked to her maiden name, led her to information linked to her previously married name. That opened a long stream of social media posts that detailed a tumultuous relationship. As she dug a little deeper, she came across a post from someone else in Ginger's circle of friends that accused her of cheating on her then husband.

The sight of that post gave Mary chills. Was that why Ginger felt guilty, because she was the one who had violated her marriage vows? According to his own admission, Travis had cheated on his wife and Jerome had been the one to prove it. If that was the case, was it possible that Jerome was somehow involved in ruining Ginger's previous marriage? Mary's heart pounded at the thought. She knew that there was only one way she could find out. She looked up the information for Jerome's business. She assumed if he was always on the road, on a case, then he must have been on a case in Garber, too, and he must have had someone to answer his phones back home. As she dialed the number, she knew it was too late for someone to be in the office, but she still hoped someone might answer. After a few rings she was about to hang up, when someone answered.

"This is Phyllis. Are you trying to reach Jerome?"

"Actually, I was trying to reach you, Phyllis, my name is Mary, and I am hoping that you can help me with something. Were you Jerome's receptionist?"

"Yes." Phyllis' voice trembled some. "Are you one of his clients?"

"No, I'm not. I live in Garber, where Jerome was visiting. I'm very sorry for your loss."

"Thank you." Phyllis took a deep breath. "It's all very shocking."

"I know it must be. I am consulting with the police, and if you wouldn't mind, I had hoped you might be able to help me with something." Mary held her breath, she hated bending the truth, but she doubted that Phyllis would be willing to reveal the details of Jerome's cases with a stranger.

"Okay, what is it?" Phyllis sighed into the phone.

"I've been trying to find out a little bit more about Jerome Poole, his history, and any family connections that I might be able to reach out to." Mary held her breath as she wasn't sure how the woman would react.

"The police have already contacted me for information. Jerome didn't have any family, at least no one close." Phyllis' voice trembled.

"I'm so sorry. I didn't mean to upset you. I know this has to be a very difficult time for you." Mary frowned. Clearly, the receptionist was close with Jerome.

"We were each other's family," Phyllis murmured. "I don't know why I'm still answering the phones. I guess, a part of me keeps hoping that I will pick up the phone one of these times and it will be him calling." She cleared her throat. "I'm sorry, I know you didn't call to talk to me about all of this."

"I don't mind at all. I know sometimes you just need someone to talk to. I'd just like to know more about Jerome, about who he really was, and the people that were in his life. So, I'm glad I've had the chance to talk to you about him." Mary bit into her bottom lip.

"It's nice to talk about him, to be honest. He loved his work. Most people would judge him for what he did, always getting into the business of other people. But it wasn't just about cheating spouses and insurance fraud. He also did extra work on the side, things to prevent crime, or help out police on investigations. He was a very curious man, and he always liked to get to the truth."

"He sounds like a wonderful person to know. Phyllis, do you know why he was here in Garber? Was he working on a case?" Mary picked up a pen to jot down any notes she might need.

"I have no idea. Like I told the police, he was working a case and then he called me to tell me he was just taking a couple of days off. I thought it was suspicious because he never takes days off. I pressed him, but he said that it was something he didn't want me involved in. He said it was too dangerous." Phyllis took a sharp breath. "I should have asked more questions. I should have made him tell me the truth."

"I'm sure you did everything you could, Phyllis. It sounds like he cared about you a lot as well."

"He did and I cared about him."

"What case was he working on?"

"I'm not sure about the details of the case but the client was Robert Prowlow. He wanted to deal directly with Jerome, so he didn't give me any details. He called Jerome directly, he got his details from a friend apparently, a previous client of Jerome's. The case was in Shorehead. But there weren't any other notes. Jerome's computer was being repaired and it was just returned to me. So, I only just managed to find Robert's name. I still need to give the details to the police."

"Do you know if he found anything there?" Mary's voice rose slightly in anticipation.

"No, like I said he didn't tell me anything, he called me after the case and said he was just going to take a couple of days off." Phyllis sighed.

"Do you know if he ever investigated someone named Ginger Halo?" Mary lowered her voice as she spoke Ginger's name.

"Ginger. Ginger." Phyllis repeated the name over and over. "I do remember a Ginger. Give me a moment." She paused. "Oh yes, I remember Ginger now. That was such an unusual case."

"Unusual? How?" Mary began to write down every word that Phyllis said.

"Normally, Jerome was very strict about handing over any information he found to his client. But in this case, he did things differently. Adam Halo is the one who hired him because he suspected his wife was cheating. But he was a very angry man, he threatened Jerome a few times. When Jerome found the proof of the affair, he decided to warn Ginger first. He was afraid that Adam might come after her." Phyllis sighed. "He didn't get paid for that case, but he did believe that he did the right thing. After he warned Ginger, she divorced Adam."

"I bet Adam was pretty angry. What happened to him?" Mary's pen hovered over the notepad in front of her.

"Adam was angry that he hadn't found any proof. He showed up at the office a few times to harass Jerome. But he passed away about a year later."

"Adam's dead?" Disappointment flooded through Mary.

"Yes, Ginger notified us when he passed. She said she didn't want us to worry anymore. Sweet woman." Phyllis sighed. "I'm sorry, Mary, I'm still feeling a little overwhelmed."

"I understand, Phyllis. Thank you for your help, and like I said I'm very sorry for your loss." Mary ended the call. Was it possible that Ginger had killed both Adam and Jerome? She didn't see a reason why she would kill Jerome, yet, but it was still possible that she would find one.

CHAPTER 17

Unable to sleep, Suzie finally tossed her blanket off and climbed out of bed. She pulled on jeans and a t-shirt, then grabbed her jacket. As she slipped out of the house, she had no plan in mind. She just needed to find out more about Travis. She walked in the direction of his house. The quiet of the late evening hour gave her some comfort, but the sound of the distant howl of a dog raised goosebumps on her arms. Perhaps it wasn't the wisest thing to be out walking alone at night, but in Garber she usually felt safe at all hours.

As Suzie neared Travis' house, she noticed a faint glow near the porch. It was a tiny pinprick of light, that glowed brighter a second later. As she drew closer, she recognized it as the tip of a cigarette. Suzie's heart skipped a beat. Was it Travis on the porch? She hadn't expected him to be awake, or outside. However, a few steps later she could make out the shape of the person. It definitely wasn't Travis. The figure was too petite to be Travis. Was it the woman he was with at the restaurant?

Suzie softened her steps as she reached the edge of the front yard. Could she spy without being spotted? From her vantage point it appeared the woman faced away from her. She decided to get just a little closer and made her way up the side of the yard. Just then the glow of a flame illuminated the woman's features. The lighter cut off a second later, but it was on long enough for Suzie to recognize the face of the woman who held it. She'd met her at Dune House. She worked at Pelicans on the Pier. Justine. Justine, on Travis' front porch in what looked like a nightgown, well after most visitors would be expected to leave for the night. Justine and Travis? Her throat tightened. Was it possible that they had been working together?

Unable to resist, Suzie walked right up to the porch.

"Justine?"

"Yes?" The young woman looked up at her with a faint scowl. "Can I help you?"

"Sorry, I was wondering if I could have one of those." Suzie pointed towards the pack of cigarettes on the table beside her.

"I guess." Justine frowned as she opened the pack. "The stores close too early around here."

"They really do." Suzie took the cigarette from her.

"Need a light?" Justine flicked the lighter on again. She narrowed her eyes at Suzie. "Wait a minute, I know you. I met you at that beautiful bed and breakfast. Sean told me all about you being nosy. Thanks to you, the police showed up at his house this evening, scared his mother so bad he thought he would have to take her to the hospital." She pursed her lips as she glared. "You don't even smoke, do you?"

"Uh, no." Suzie offered the cigarette back. "I just wanted a chance to talk to you."

"I don't have a thing to say to you." Justine turned and started towards the front door of the house.

"Justine, wait." Suzie stepped towards her. "I don't mean any harm. I'm just trying to find out what happened at the restaurant." Her heart pounded as she prepared to use a technique that she knew could work in certain situations but could also backfire in others. "I'm hearing stories from someone else. Don't you want your side to be heard before the police find out?"

"My side?" Justine spun around suddenly. "My side of what?"

"Your side of what happened to Jerome." Suzie locked her eyes to Justine's. "Somehow that poison got in his food, Justine, and people certainly have theories."

"Theories about me?" Justine's eyes widened. She took a few steps towards Suzie. "That's impossible."

"Unfortunately, it's not. Everyone in that restaurant that night is a suspect. Especially those that had access to the kitchen." Suzie focused on the subtle twitch of Justine's facial features. Her brows furrowed with concern.

"I was nowhere near Jerome's food." Justine crossed her arms.

"So, you never went into the kitchen while it was being prepared?"

"Of course, I went into the kitchen, but that doesn't mean anything." Justine scowled.

"I'm guessing that Travis and his girlfriend broke up after that scene with Jerome at Cheney's?

Is that why he asked you to help him get rid of Jerome?" Suzie shook her head.

"Quiet!" Justine glared straight into her eyes. "I had nothing to do with any of this, and neither did Travis."

"Justine?" Travis pushed open the front door and peered out. "Who's out there with you?"

"A nosy neighbor." Justine glanced at Travis. "She's here to accuse us of murder!"

"Suzie?" Travis stepped out onto the porch. "Is that you?"

"It is." Suzie's heart raced. Things had certainly backfired. Justine was not about to confess, and the anger in Travis' eyes made her think she should run.

"Get off my property. Get away from here and stay away. I've already been cleared by the police, I'm not afraid to report harassment." Travis pointed at her. "You need to stay out of this before you make things much worse for yourself."

"I'm going, I'm going." Suzie held up her hands as she took a step back.

"I prefer if you don't spread this around. There is nothing to our meeting," Justine snapped. "We just ran into each other today and decided to keep each other company. If you want to use that to try to prove I'm a murderer, it's not going to work, and you're going to look like a fool."

"Get out of here." Travis scowled. "I'm not going to warn you again."

Suzie hurried back to the sidewalk. Frustrated, and a little embarrassed, she hurried back to Dune House. There was still a possibility that Justine could have been involved, but the young woman was right, she didn't have a single shred of proof.

CHAPTER 18

Mary awoke the next morning to the sound of footsteps in the hallway outside her room. She took a sharp breath as she heard the scuff of another shoe. It wasn't often that anyone woke up before she did. Pilot snored next to her. A quick glance at the clock on her bedside table revealed that she hadn't overslept. It would still be thirty minutes until her alarm went off, which it rarely had the chance to. As she swung her legs over the side of the bed, she felt a familiar twinge of pain. Mornings were not kind to her anymore, but after moving around for a bit, she knew the pain level would become tolerable. Unfortunately, if she wanted to find out who was in the hallway, she would have to move quickly. She gritted her teeth against the pain and managed to pull open the door seconds later. In the hall she spotted Ginger with her suitcase in hand.

"Ginger? Where are you off to?"

"Oh, we're checking out, dear. I didn't want to wake you. We want to get an early start." Ginger shifted the suitcase from one hand to the other.

"You should stay for the day." Mary stepped farther out of her room. "It's going to be a perfect beach day."

"I think it's best if we go. We have to get back to reality sometime." Ginger smiled. "Thanks for being so accommodating, we really enjoyed our time here."

"At least let me make you breakfast. I know that you didn't want to eat here during your stay, but I make these cinnamon rolls that are sure to get you through your long drive. It's a quick recipe. I promise, you won't regret it." Mary met Ginger's eyes and hoped the woman would agree. She knew that Jason would need all of the time he could get before the couple left Garber.

"Actually, that sounds delicious. Thank you." Ginger smiled. "Maybe we'll take a quick walk on the beach while you're baking. It is so beautiful out there."

"Great idea." Mary nodded. "It shouldn't take long to get everything prepared." She stepped back into her room and grabbed a robe. There wasn't time to dress properly. If she wanted to be sure that the couple stuck around, she would have to make the best cinnamon rolls ever. Luckily, she really did have a fantastic, fast recipe. On her way to the kitchen, she heard Suzie coming down the stairs.

"Morning Suzie." Mary glanced over her shoulder to be sure that Ginger was out of earshot, then looked back at her. "Ginger and Sam are planning to leave. You should call Jason and let him know. In fact, invite him to breakfast, that way he can question them one last time if he wants to."

"Good idea." Suzie grabbed her phone from the pocket of her robe. "Do you need help with breakfast?"

"No, I can handle it, but if you want to take Pilot out, I'm sure he's dying for a walk." Mary stepped around the dog who eagerly followed her every move.

"I can do that. Let me just toss on some clothes." Suzie put the phone to her ear as she hurried back to her room.

"Here buddy." Mary gave Pilot a few treats, then she turned her attention to the recipe book that rested on a stand. She didn't need it. She knew the recipe by heart. But she loved the feel of the pages, and the scents that had become trapped between the covers over the years. She'd made this recipe for her children so often as they were growing up that they still requested it as adults. She knew they planned to continue the baking tradition with their own children.

When Suzie returned to the kitchen, she had jeans and a sweatshirt on. She grabbed Pilot's leash and clipped it onto his collar.

"Jason is on his way." Suzie placed a light kiss on Mary's cheek as Pilot eagerly dragged her towards the door. "I'll be right outside if you need me."

"You'll probably run into Ginger and Sam, they planned to take a walk on the beach." Mary raised an eyebrow.

"I'll make sure I do." Suzie winked at her.

Mary turned back to her baking. A few minutes later she heard the front door open and close, and Jason's familiar voice called out to her.

"Good morning, Mary."

"Good morning, Jason." She smiled as she kneaded the dough for the cinnamon rolls. "So glad you could join us."

"I wouldn't miss it." Jason sniffed the air. "I can already smell the cinnamon. Where are your guests?"

"On the beach. Suzie is also taking Pilot for a walk."

"I did find something interesting from the information you gave me. Robert Prowlow, the man that apparently hired Jerome in Shorehead, is Ginger's boss. I still don't know what the case was about, and I haven't been able to contact him, yet."

"That's interesting. Can you keep Ginger and Sam here?" Mary turned back to the dough.

"No, I don't know exactly what he was investigating in Shorehead. If she was trying to hide something why would she recommend Jerome to her boss? Ginger and Sam's address checked out, it's where Sam works. I can only insist that they are contactable if I need to speak to them, they don't live very far away. Unfortunately, there's nothing strong enough to keep them here." Jason leaned against the counter beside her. "Though that may be for the best. If they're not guilty of the crime, there's no reason to keep them here."

"Even with their past connection to Jerome?" Mary began to roll the dough into buns.

"It surprised me to hear about it, but so far it

hasn't led to anything incriminating. If anything, I'd say that Jerome did her a favor back then. I don't see why she would be harboring any animosity now." Jason frowned. "Unless she had something new to hide. Maybe when Ginger saw Jerome was in town, she thought he was investigating her again, and decided she had to get rid of him?"

"I hadn't thought about that." Mary frowned as she turned to look at him. "What would she have to hide? Do you think she's cheating on Sam?"

"Well." Jason shrugged. "I have heard that cheating can often be a hard habit to break. Maybe she is, and maybe she thought that was why Jerome was here."

"I think if it was why he was here, his recep-tionist would have known about that." Mary sighed as she slid the tray of cinnamon rolls into the oven. "She said that Jerome seemed frightened of what he was involved in, as if he thought it was too dangerous for her to even know about. I can't see a cheating scandal as being dangerous."

"Neither can I, but it's still a possibility." Jason glanced towards the door. "I think I'll see if I can catch up with them on the beach."

"The cinnamon rolls should be ready in about twenty minutes." Mary nodded to him, then picked up a small mixing bowl. "See what you can figure out, I've got frosting to whip up."

"Wow, now you've got my mouth watering." Jason groaned, then flashed her a grin as he stepped out through the side door in the dining room.

Mary turned back to the stove as a sense of dread washed over her. She always enjoyed making her favorite cinnamon rolls, but this time, there was nothing to celebrate.

CHAPTER 19

*P*ilot tugged Suzie along the beach. She saw why within a few seconds. Ginger and Sam were a few feet ahead of them, their hands intertwined, and their heads leaned close together. The two appeared like any other couple strolling along the beach, content with each other, and enamored with the beauty around them. As Suzie watched them, she tried to picture either one of them putting poison into Jerome's mashed potatoes. Did either of them have it in them to be a murderer? She'd learned long ago that a killer didn't look a certain way, a criminal couldn't be pinpointed by a common description, people who did horrible things came in all shapes and sizes, all ages and from all walks of life. But these two?

Pilot barked, alerting the couple to his presence.

Ginger turned to face Suzie and smiled.

"I didn't know you were there." She waved to her. "Come join us. It's such a beautiful morning."

Suzie smiled in return and caught up with them.

"It is so nice out, isn't it?" She glanced at Sam. "Mary said you two are heading out. Such a shame when the weather is so beautiful."

"Enough trying to con us into staying." Sam frowned. "It's a long drive home. Besides, after what happened here, it feels wrong to enjoy our time here."

"Ah, I can understand that." Suzie nodded. "It is such a tragedy to be faced with."

"We were faced with it." Sam locked his eyes to hers. "Ginger and I were right there, at the same table with the poor fellow. I mean, how do you get over something like that? Sure, he may have been a stranger to us, but that doesn't mean it wasn't shocking."

"But he wasn't a stranger to you, was he?" Jason's words drifted over Suzie's shoulder.

"Detective Allen." Ginger jumped at the sight of him. "I didn't realize you were behind me."

"Sorry, I came for breakfast, and spotted all of you out here." Jason narrowed his eyes as he looked at Ginger. "Jerome wasn't a stranger to you, was he Ginger?"

"What are you talking about?" Sam crossed his arms as he stared at Jason. "Why are you speaking to her like that?"

"Sam. Could you give us a minute." Ginger glanced over at him. "Please?"

"There's nothing that you need to say that I shouldn't hear." Sam looped his arm through hers.

"There is something that I'd rather not discuss with you right now." Ginger looked into his eyes. "Please."

"Ginger?" Sam stared at her.

"I will tell you everything, Sam, but not like this." Ginger took a deep breath. "Just give me a few minutes."

"Fine." Sam frowned as he stepped away from her. He walked along the water but glanced back over his shoulder at her.

"I guess you figured it out, huh?" Ginger looked back at Jason. "I assumed that you would, eventually."

"I can't take the credit for it, but yes I am aware that you and Jerome had a past connection. In fact, he investigated your previous marriage."

"Then you should also be aware that Jerome

didn't do anything to hurt me. In fact, he helped me." Ginger closed her eyes, then shook her head. "That was so long ago. I like to pretend it was a different lifetime. If it wasn't for Jerome telling me about the investigation, I would have lost everything, maybe even my life. He was worried about my safety, so he warned me." She bit into her bottom lip and took a sharp breath. "He was a good man, who didn't deserve any of this."

"Did you keep in contact with him over the years?" Suzie met her eyes. "Did you recognize him?"

"On and off we did. I referred a few of my friends to him when they had issues, they needed solved. I even referred my boss to him, he said he needed someone to investigate something for him. Jerome and I weren't close friends or anything. We never even met in person, but I never forgot what he did for me." Ginger rocked back on her heels. "I sent him a letter recently, to thank him, again. Finding Sam has been like my second chance at life, at love, and I only have it because of what Jerome did for me. I wasn't sure where to send the letter to, but I had some time off and my boss mentioned that whatever he was investigating led Jerome to Garber. That's when I decided to have a break here and thank him in person, instead."

"That's why you insisted on staying at Dune House?" Suzie nodded. "Even though Sam wasn't so thrilled."

"We needed a vacation, and the truth is, I needed to tell him about my past. I thought maybe once I spoke to Jerome, I'd be ready to tell Sam about my mistakes. It seemed like the right way to do things. I was going to speak to Jerome right after dinner. But I never got the chance." Ginger ran her hands across her face and sighed. "I know how this must look. I know that it all seems too coincidental, but I didn't have anything to do with killing Jerome." She lowered her hands and looked straight at Jason. "You don't have to believe me, but it's the truth. If I knew who hurt Jerome, I'd be more than happy to tell you. But we were all just eating, enjoying our meals, and then Jerome was gone. I know I still need to tell Sam about what happened, but with everything else going on, it just didn't seem like the right time."

"Do you know why Jerome came to Garber? What he was investigating?" Jason frowned. "Did your boss tell you? I haven't been able to get hold of him."

"No, not at all. He wanted to keep it under wraps. I have no idea if it was personal or business related." Ginger glanced back at Sam, who watched her from the water's edge. "I wish there was more I could tell you, but that is honestly all I know." She frowned. "You can arrest me if you want, but it won't change anything."

"I'm not going to arrest you." Jason ran his hand along the back of his neck. "I have no reason to. I appreciate your cooperation. I will be in touch if I have more questions."

"Okay." Ginger looked at Suzie. "I need to get back to Sam before he decides to give up on me. I just hope that when I tell him the truth he doesn't decide to walk away."

"If he can't handle the truth, then he might not be the right person for you." Suzie looked past her, at Sam, then back to Ginger. "But if you never give him the chance, you'll never know for sure."

"You're right." Ginger smiled some. "Thanks Suzie." She turned and walked off towards Sam.

"Isn't there anything we can do to find out for sure why Jerome was here?" Suzie fell into step beside Jason as they both headed back in the direction of Dune House.

"I've been trying. I searched his hotel room,

cataloged everything we could find in his rental car. I documented every store and restaurant he visited based on his credit card activity, as well as canvassing the local businesses with his picture. But none of it pieces anything together for me. As far as his actions go, it was as if he was on a vacation. He ate out, he bought snacks to have at the hotel, he visited the museum, the library." Jason shrugged.

"The library?" Suzie raised an eyebrow. "That seems a little odd. What about his computer or his cell phone?"

"He didn't have a cell phone on him, or in his car, or at his hotel. He came to Garber with one, we were able to trace his last call from it to the docks, not far from Dune House. But after that there isn't any activity. There was no computer either. Apparently, his computer was being repaired. A couple of officers have picked it up and they are going through it now." Jason shrugged. "I thought maybe he'd decided to take a break from technology and not bring with a replacement computer, but where did his phone go?"

"Interesting." Suzie followed him into Dune House with Pilot at her side.

Mary turned to face Suzie and Jason as they stepped into the house.

"Nice walk?" Mary smiled as she set the tray of cinnamon rolls on the counter to cool slightly.

"Very nice." Suzie sniffed the air. "Wow, I wish I could smell that scent forever."

"Oh, you'd get sick of it, eventually." Mary grinned.

"No, I don't think I would." Suzie walked over to her and leaned close to the cinnamon rolls.

"Don't touch, they're cooling a bit so I can put the frosting on." Mary winked at her, then looked straight at Jason. "Did you speak to Ginger?"

"Yes, I did." Jason sat down at the dining room table. "Unfortunately, our conversation didn't lead to anything new."

"Coffee is ready." Mary carried the pot to the table where several coffee mugs were already placed out. "I'm guessing you could use some of this."

"You guessed right." Jason nodded and smiled as she poured some into a mug near him. "Thanks Mary."

"You're welcome." Mary filled a mug for herself and Suzie as well. "Where are Sam and Ginger now?"

"Having an uncomfortable conversation, I'd guess." Suzie sat down across from Jason. "She planned to confess the truth about her previous marriage."

"That will be tough." Mary sat down with them as well. "It's funny isn't it? The ways our lives change. There was never a time when I thought I'd be running a bed and breakfast with you, Suzie, and now I can't imagine living any other way."

"Me either." Suzie took a sip of her coffee.

"I wonder if Jerome's life changed that way." Jason rapped his knuckles on the table. "Maybe things in his life took a dark turn, one so dark that he couldn't share it with the people around him."

"According to his receptionist, that could be very possible." Mary nodded slowly. "She said he wouldn't tell her what was going on because it was too dangerous."

"I think the key to solving this might be taking a closer look at Jerome's activities while he was here. We need to find out exactly what brought him to Garber." Suzie narrowed her eyes. "It may be the key to figuring out who was after him. He must have been on to something that someone was willing to murder to hide."

"I need to talk to Ginger's boss." Jason's eyes narrowed. "Whatever Jerome was working on in Shorehead for him, might hold the key to this."

"Oh wow, that smells delicious." Ginger nearly squealed as she stepped through the side door off the dining room. Sam followed right behind her, his hand wrapped around hers. "Mary, you weren't kidding about your specialty."

"No, I wasn't." Mary grinned as she stood up. "There's fresh coffee, I just have to frost the cinnamon rolls and they will be ready to eat."

"Can't wait." Sam pulled out a chair for Ginger, and once she was settled, he sat down beside her. Immediately, he took her hand again.

Suzie noticed the way he looked over at Ginger, his lips curved in a faint smile. If they'd had their conversation, it seemed to her that it had gone quite well. She thought about how it felt when Paul took her hand. It was such a simple gesture, something that she'd experienced many times in her life, but when Paul's hand curled around hers, it stirred something unexpected in her every single time, a subtle sense of surprise, and contentment. She sensed the same reaction in Ginger as she turned to smile at Sam. No, she didn't have anything to worry about with Sam. She had no reason to want to kill Jerome. At least, none that Suzie could see.

Mary poured two more mugs of coffee, then focused on the cinnamon rolls. Minutes later she returned to the table with the tray and everyone dug in.

"I'd better get back to it." Jason wiped his mouth with a napkin and stood up from the table. He gave Pilot a quick pat. "Sam, Ginger, have a safe trip home." He nodded to them, then turned and walked out the door.

Pilot trailed after him to the door, then lay down not far from it.

"I can't thank you enough for your hospitality." Ginger gave Mary a hug, then Suzie. "Maybe our little vacation didn't go exactly as planned, but I am grateful we came just the same."

After they left, Mary began to pack up the remaining cinnamon rolls.

"Some for Wes, and some for Paul?" She smiled as she piled them into two separate paper sacks.

"Wonderful. I know that Paul will love them." Suzie carried the empty tray to the sink and began to wash it. "I can't stop thinking about exactly what Jerome was doing here. Jason said they didn't find a computer, or his cell phone. How could he conduct an investigation with no tools to do any research with?" She shook her head. "When I conducted investigations, I had my computer, my phone, my contacts in different areas, I used all of them. The only thing that I can think is that maybe he used the computers at the library. Jason said he went there a few times."

"If so, they might still have a record of what he was researching." Mary wiped her hands on a dish towel. "Let's head over there and find out what Louis might know."

"Good idea." Suzie grabbed one of the paper bags. "I can drop this off to Paul on the way back."

As they headed out the door, Pilot gave a soft whimper.

"Not this time, buddy." Mary smiled as she crouched down to pet him. "No dogs in the library. I know, I know, it's not fair." She scratched behind his ear, then followed Suzie out the door.

CHAPTER 20

*A*s Suzie and Mary walked towards the library, Mary watched the people they walked past. Everyone had gotten back into their usual routines, and yet things still felt foreign to her. A terrible crime had taken place in their beautiful town, and though she knew that people had to move on, she couldn't quite understand how they had been able to. Maybe she would be able to feel the same way once Jerome's killer had been found.

Suzie opened the door to the library and they both stepped inside. The air-conditioned environment always had the same faint scent of paper and glue. Mary smiled as it wafted under her nose.

"Ladies." Louis smiled at them as they approached the central desk. "It's good to see you."

He sniffed the air. "Did you bring me something delicious?"

"Oh sure." Suzie smiled as she pulled one of the cinnamon rolls from the paper bag she held. "Mary made them this morning."

"Yum. Thank you so much." Louis took a big bite of the cinnamon roll.

"Jason mentioned that Jerome had been in here a few times during his stay in Garber. We were just wondering if you noticed whether he used the computers?" Suzie closed up the bag.

"Yes, he did. He said his computer was being repaired. I had to log him in because he didn't have a library card." Louis pointed to one of the computers along the wall. "He used that one." He raised an eyebrow. "If you happened to login you would probably still be able to access his history."

"Thanks Louis." Suzie headed for the computer.

Mary leaned against the counter as she looked at Louis. "Did he say anything to you about why he was here?"

"No, he didn't say much at all. Just came in, sat at the computer for about an hour, printed off a few things, and then left. He did that for about two or three days in a row." Louis shrugged. "I didn't think anything of it at the time."

"Any idea what he printed?" Mary met his eyes.

"That I couldn't tell you. It was only a few pages, though." Louis took another bite of his cinnamon roll. "This is delicious."

"Thanks." Mary smiled at him, then walked over to join Suzie at the computer. "Anything interesting?"

"He spent a lot of time on this site." Suzie tilted the monitor some so that Mary could see as well. "From what I can tell it gives information about the docks, about the boats available to charter, and the daily activity to be expected in the area."

"Look at this." Mary pointed to a small image on the upper right-hand corner of the screen. "It links to a live video feed of the dock."

"Let's see." Suzie clicked it, then waited as the image loaded. "Not much to see." She watched as the water lapped at the dock and the boats rocked gently back and forth.

"Not now there isn't." Mary glanced at her watch. "It's fairly early still. Can you tell when he accessed the site?"

"Uh, let's see." Suzie frowned as she skimmed through the history tab. "No unfortunately, it just has dates, not times."

"Well, he might have been looking for something." Mary pulled up a chair beside her.

"Maybe, but we don't even know for sure if he clicked on this link. The only thing we can be certain about is that he definitely had an interest in the dock, and what was happening there." Suzie flipped through a few more websites. "The rest are just news sites."

"News sites? Local news?" Mary leaned forward.

"No, actually. Local news sites for a city in New York." Suzie shook her head. "I'm not sure why he would be looking that up. It looks like he read a few articles about a crime family there. The Mennossi family."

"I bet that's what he printed out." Mary shrugged. "But why?"

"Whatever he was investigating might have been related to this crime family somehow." Suzie skimmed the article on the monitor. "I don't see how it could be related to Garber, but something might connect it." She frowned. "Let me look a little further into this." As she began to type, she heard Mary's phone buzz with a text.

"Oops, I forgot to turn the volume down." Mary glanced around the library guiltily as she dug her phone out of her purse. She was relieved to see that Louis was on a phone call and hadn't heard it.

"Don't worry, we're the only ones here." Suzie smiled, then scrolled through the results of her search.

"Oh, look at this." Mary handed her phone over to Suzie. "Phyllis sent a list of Jerome's most recent clients and information about the investigations he conducted for them."

"Wow, this is a lot of information." Suzie began to sort through it. "There are so many names, he definitely didn't have a shortage of work. I'll see what I can find." She rolled her chair away from the computer. "See if you can find anything else in his history that might explain his connection to Garber."

Mary pulled a chair over in front of the computer and sat down. She pressed at the keys as she attempted a few different searches. After some time slipped by, she shook her head. "I'm sorry, Suzie, but I'm not finding much of anything. How about you?"

"This is rather pointless." Suzie set the phone down and sighed as she sat back in her chair. "We want to believe that we're going to find an answer in his past, but it's like searching for a needle in a haystack. Any number of his past clients could have held enough of a grudge to want him dead. Whatever he was doing here in Garber, we're not going to find it by spending hours on a computer. I think we're better off looking at our suspects. We know someone here in Garber killed him."

"Maybe." Mary turned around in her chair and frowned. "Could we track down which of his clients might have been in Garber at the time of the murder? I can at least go through this list, make some calls, and find out where each person might have been at the time of his death."

"That will take days, if not weeks." Suzie shook her head. "And it will only lead somewhere if the people you call are willing to answer your questions. Let's not forget that the nature of a private eye's investigations is often secretive. Half of these people, if not more, probably never want to hear from or about him again. We can't just keep sifting through an endless cycle of answering machines and hang-ups."

"What else do you suggest?" Mary looked up at her. "We don't have much else to go on."

"Not yet, we don't. We do know that the chef was in the kitchen and prepared the tainted mashed potatoes. We know that the waiter served him the tainted mashed potatoes. We also know that at least one man in our community had a reason to want him dead. Not to mention Freddy, a shady stranger who just happens to be in town at the time of his death and seated right next to him at the table before he died. I'd say that we have plenty of suspects to work with right here in Garber." Suzie sat forward in her chair again. "They are the ones that most likely had the opportunity to kill him. They are the ones we should concentrate on."

"You really don't think we should investigate any of these other people?" Mary took her phone back.

"Let the police sort through them. I'm sure that Jason has the information, but I'll make sure he gets this information just in case, and he has the manpower to comb through this computer history a lot better than we can."

"That's true." Mary nodded. "With Ginger and Sam gone, we have a few less suspects, unless new evidence comes to light. Maybe it's time to narrow down the suspect list some more."

"I think our first stop should be the chef. His kitchen was the source of the poison, at least, we can assume that for now until we are able to prove otherwise." Suzie stood up and waved briefly to

Louis. "Maybe Jason will be able to come up with something from the computer, or this list of clients. But until then we should keep asking questions."

Mary pushed her chair under the table, then looked at Suzie. "Why don't you let me talk to the chef?"

"Okay." Suzie met her eyes and smiled. "Maybe you can share your cinnamon roll recipe with him, that would definitely win him over."

"Speaking of cinnamon rolls." Mary tipped her head towards the paper bag in Suzie's hand. "They're not going to be nearly as good if you wait much longer."

"Good point." Suzie smiled. "I guess it's time to pay Paul a visit. Maybe he can give me some insight into what Jerome might have been looking for on those cameras."

CHAPTER 21

*M*ary waved to Suzie as she headed off towards Pelicans on the Pier. She'd heard rumors that the restaurant planned to reopen that evening, or maybe the next day. She guessed that if that were the case, she might be able to find the chef there preparing food for the reopening. It made her stomach churn to think of the restaurant opening again so soon, but she also knew that if the restaurant had any chance of surviving it had to reopen. Would they really use the same chef? Would anyone be willing to eat there? With these thoughts on her mind she approached the front door of the restaurant. Mary was about to open it, when the door pushed open from the inside. A young woman stepped out. Mary recognized her straight away from when she visited Dune House.

"Hannah."

"Hi there." She met Mary's eyes. "I remember you from that bed and breakfast, Dune House."

"Mary." She offered her a smile. "I was wondering if I could speak to your chef."

"He's inside." Hannah continued to block the doorway. "Why do you want to speak to him?"

"I'm curious about a recipe I heard he created. I thought maybe I could check the ingredients with him, but I haven't been able to contact him. I'd really like to speak to him. I'm hoping to make the recipe for a special guest arriving soon." Mary searched the woman's eyes. Would she believe her story, or would she see right through it?

"All right." Hannah nodded as she stepped inside. "He's preparing for our reopening tonight."

"So, the rumors are true." Mary started to step through the door. "I wish you luck with that."

"Thanks." Hannah sighed. "We're definitely going to need it."

Mary made her way to the kitchen. As she walked through the dining room, she noticed the arrangement of the tables. She hadn't noticed it properly the first night as it had been so busy. There were at least twenty chairs at each long table. It did give the environment a homey feel, but the knowledge of what happened to Jerome there, tainted it. She pushed the door open to the kitchen and stepped inside.

"Excuse me, are you busy?"

"Always." The chef glanced over at her, his eyes narrowed. "Do you need something?"

"Just to speak with you for a few minutes." Mary allowed the door to swing closed behind her. "I wasn't sure if you'd still be working here, Cody."

"I'm cheap labor. I've worked in plenty of restaurants." Cody shrugged and shifted the bag of carrots onto the cutting board. "I've seen them open, I've seen them succeed, I've seen them struggle, and I've seen them fail." He pulled a carrot out of the bag, then picked up a long, wide knife. The overhead light glinted off the spotless blade as he held it over the carrot. "I don't get attached."

"You go where the money leads you, hmm?" Mary smiled as she watched the knife hover.

"You could say that." Cody sliced the knife down through the carrot with a sharp motion.

"Already, they're ready to reopen. Doesn't that

worry you?" Mary glanced around the kitchen, then back at him. "I'm sure that after what happened, you could use some time to recover."

"It's all right. I have to pay the bills." Cody set the knife down and settled his piercing gaze on her. "Why don't you just drop the small talk and ask me what you want to ask me."

"I just asked for a tour of the kitchen." Mary shrugged, as her heartbeat quickened. "There's nothing strange about that."

"Not at all." Cody's fingers remained wrapped around the handle of the knife. "Except, I know that's not why you're here. I heard you say you needed a recipe, but you haven't mentioned that since you've been in the kitchen. I know that you're not interested in a tour of the kitchen. So, Mary was it?" He narrowed his eyes as she nodded. "Ask me what you really want to know."

"I don't have anything to ask you." Mary looked from him, to the knife, and all at once recognized just how isolated the kitchen was from the rest of the restaurant. Obviously, he had been listening in on her conversation since the moment she arrived. He was on edge. He could easily attack her before anyone had the chance to hear her call for help. "I didn't mean to disturb you." She began to back up towards the door.

"Ask me, did I poison that poor man?" The blade of the knife scraped across the counter as he adjusted his position so that he could face her. "Did I pour poison into his mashed potatoes, and mix it up all nice?" A wicked smile spread across his lips.

"I have no idea what you're talking about." Mary's heart pounded. Her mind spun with a mixture of panic and disgust.

"Sure, you don't." Cody shook his head and turned back to the carrot on the counter. "I didn't kill anyone, Mary. Not that it matters. The suspicion will hover over me until the real killer is caught." He sliced another piece of carrot. "My career is ruined. I have a job here because the owner couldn't get another chef to walk in here, but this restaurant won't stay open long. I'll have to beg and hope that someone will take pity on me." He pointed the knife at her as he continued to speak. "You don't know humility until you see that look in someone's eyes."

"I'm sorry for your troubles." Mary winced the moment the knife pointed in her direction. "But I didn't cause them. A man lost his life, and everyone has a lot of questions."

"Maybe, but I'm not the cause of it. Perhaps people should stop trying to blame me." Cody tipped his head towards the door. "Go on, go pick out a table. I'll make you something special." He chuckled. "Oh wait, I guess you probably weren't planning on eating."

Mary gritted her teeth as she walked out of the kitchen. He claimed that he had nothing to do with the crime, but his attitude left her wondering if he might have been involved after all.

⁓

*S*uzie stepped onto Paul's boat and smiled as he turned to face her.

"I brought you something." She held out the bag to him.

"Oh, Mary's cinnamon rolls?" Paul grinned as he opened the bag and took a big sniff. "Wow, thank you so much."

"You're welcome." Suzie hugged him. "Sorry they're not warmer. Mary and I stopped by the library to see if we could figure out what Jerome was investigating while he was here. About the only thing it led to was the live camera feed that's on the dock here."

"Oh?" Paul raised an eyebrow. "I wonder why he was looking that up."

"I'm not sure." Suzie frowned, then leaned back against the outside of the cabin of the boat. "I keep hoping that something will pop up to give me some direction, but I just end up with bits and pieces that don't fit together. Jerome was interested in a crime family that operated hundreds of miles away. What could that have to do with Garber?"

"I don't know." Paul ran his hand back through his hair. "Maybe he was tracking one of the members?"

"Maybe." Suzie crossed her arms as she looked out over the dock. "So many people come and go through here. Jason said there has been an increase in out-of-towners. Have you noticed that?"

"Not really. I mean, on the weekends we get some out of town charter boats, or those that have heard it's a good spot to fish, but during the week it's usually just the regulars. The only person out of the ordinary that I've noticed, is Freddy. He's still hanging around, too." Paul narrowed his eyes. "I saw him with a couple of guys this morning. They weren't locals, that's for sure."

"What made you think that?" Suzie met his eyes.

"The way they were dressed. Suits, long jackets,

it looked like they were dressed for a funeral, not for a day on a boat, and certainly not for a stroll around Garber. No one here is that formal." Paul shrugged. "I just got a strange feeling about the whole thing. But then I've had a strange feeling about Freddy since the first time I saw him."

"Freddy might have some seedy connections we're not aware of, interesting." Suzie leaned into Paul's shoulder and took a deep breath of the salty air as it coasted off the water. "I've been trying to find anything about him that would make me second guess my instincts that he's up to no good, but so far I haven't been able to find much at all."

"Maybe he's just a private person?" Paul wrapped his arm around her shoulders. "Maybe there's not much out there to find."

"It's possible. But it just makes me wonder why?" Suzie looked into Paul's eyes. "I'm not one to blather on about my personal life on social media, but I do post things now and then, especially for the business."

"Never about me." Paul quirked an eyebrow as he looked at her. "I've noticed."

"You have?" Suzie frowned and straightened up. "I didn't realize."

"Don't worry." Paul grinned as he pulled Suzie

close again. "I like it. I think our business, should be our business. I don't really understand why everyone is so quick to post pictures of their breakfast, lunch, and dinner. I certainly don't need to see pictures of us parading around the internet."

"Good to know." Suzie smiled as she stroked his cheek. "But Freddy's quite a bit younger than us. I think it's just a little unusual that he has such a small digital footprint."

"Maybe you're not looking in the right places?" Paul tipped his head to the side as he studied her. "You think Freddy is a criminal to start with. Maybe that has colored your investigative technique."

"Listen to you." Suzie laughed as she gazed at him. "Critiquing my methods."

"Never." Paul shifted against the railing so that he could face her. "I would never critique anything about you, Suzie." He smiled. "I just hate to see you frustrated, and since I know that if there is something to know about Freddy, you are the person that will be able to find it, I thought I'd offer a little advice."

"It's not terrible advice, I suppose." Suzie smiled as she searched his eyes. "Maybe I did assume too quickly."

"Only one way to find out." Paul leaned in for a

kiss. Suzie warmed to the touch of his lips, to the attentive way he stroked her cheek with his fingertips, but her thoughts remained on Freddy, and on the murder that she wanted to solve. As if he could sense it, Paul pulled back and looked at her. "I guess I'll see you tomorrow? You've already disappeared back into the case."

"At least I brought you cinnamon rolls to keep you warm." Suzie winked at him.

"They're cold, Suzie." Paul called out to her as she climbed off the boat. "But I'll still enjoy them."

"I know you will." Suzie smiled, then hurried down the dock towards the main office. If Freddy had chartered a boat, and taken it out with friends, she might at least be able to find out where they went and how long they planned to be gone. Maybe Freddy was a legitimate business man that wanted to start an operation out of Garber. If that was the case, she guessed it would be fairly easy for her to prove.

Before she could reach the office however, she noticed footfalls behind her. They were timed almost to match her own. She glanced over her shoulder expecting that it might be Paul. Instead she spotted Freddy, his eyes locked to the wooden plank beneath his shoes, and his approach towards her still steady. He wasn't out on a boat at all. Was he following her? Suzie pushed the thought away. Of course, he wasn't, he had business on the dock. Tempted to ask him some questions she started to turn to face him, but something about his determined gait made her change her mind. Instead she felt the sudden urge to get away.

CHAPTER 22

*M*ary pulled back the curtains to the front window that overlooked the parking lot and the road that ran in front of Dune House. She wasn't sure when Suzie would be back, but she hoped that it would be soon. After her encounter with Chef Shouder, she didn't like the idea of being at Dune House all alone. She smiled with some relief as she spotted Suzie on her way towards the house. Then she noticed someone else a few steps behind her.

"Freddy?" Mary leaned closer to the window as she watched Suzie turn and hurry up the walkway to the front porch of Dune House. The man behind her looked up at the house, hesitated a moment, then continued to walk past the entrance of the parking lot.

Suzie burst through the front door.

"Mary?" Suzie rushed into the living room. "Is he still out there?"

"He just walked past." Mary looked over at her. "Was that Freddy?"

"Yes. I'm pretty sure he followed me." Suzie peered through the living room window, her breath expelled in short bursts. "I've never felt nervous walking back from the dock alone, but this time, I did. I wasn't sure if I was going to make it here."

"Suzie." Mary peeked out the window as well. "That must have been so frightening. What do you think he wants?"

"I don't know exactly, but as soon as I got close to Dune House, he kept walking, as if he was never following me in the first place. But I still think he was." Suzie stepped back from the window and took a deep breath. "Maybe I'm just being paranoid."

"I don't think so." Mary narrowed her eyes. "I saw him look towards the window. I bet he was checking to see if anyone was watching him."

"Did he see you?" Suzie's eyes widened.

"I'm not sure." Mary squeezed her hands

together. "I don't think he did. But maybe he spotted me and decided to continue on."

"Maybe. We can't be too careful." Suzie frowned as she began to pace across the carpet, one way, and then back the other.

"Suzie, let me get you some tea." Mary felt the draw of the comfort of the kitchen. There she could make everything better with a pinch of this and a dash of that.

"No." Suzie's fingers wrapped around Mary's. "If he's going to follow me, then I think we should follow him back. It's time we figured out exactly what Freddy is up to. He's one of our main suspects, and we still hardly know anything about him. If we can at least get an idea of where he's going, then we might find a clue as to what his intentions in Garber are."

"All right." Mary nodded. "I can tell you about Chef Shouder on the way."

"Please do." Suzie grabbed her keys from the hook by the door. "Just in case. I'm sure he has to have a car around here somewhere."

"You're right." Mary opened the front door and pointed at the street that ran in front of the parking lot of Dune House. "That's him, isn't it?" She squinted at the figure in the car.

"Yes, I think it is!" Suzie gasped as a gold sedan drove by Dune House. "We have to hurry if we're going to catch up with him."

"I'm right behind you." Mary followed her down the steps of the front porch and out into the parking lot. As they reached the car, the gold sedan stopped at the traffic light at the end of the road.

"We can still catch him." Suzie jumped into the car and started the engine.

Mary did her best to move just as quickly.

Suzie steered the car onto the road and managed to trail after the gold sedan, which remained a few car lengths ahead.

"Maybe we should call Jason." Mary crossed her arms as she looked through the windshield at Freddy's car. "It's not a good idea for us to tail him without backup."

"It might not be, but if we call Jason and wait for him, we'll lose him." Suzie shook her head as she sped up a little bit. "No, I want to know what this guy is up to once and for all. If he was following me, I want to know why, before he comes after me again."

"Don't get so close." Mary frowned as she watched the taillights through the windshield. "He'll realize he's being followed."

"I've never been out this way before." Suzie glanced at the signs they passed. "It's so desolate."

"Not completely." Mary pointed to a tall sign in the distance. "That must be some kind of truck stop. Which means the highway can't be far from here."

"You're probably right." Suzie shifted forward some in her seat and slowed the car down. "But I have no idea how to get to it."

"He's probably going to the truck stop." Mary tugged at the seatbelt that rested too snugly across her shoulder. "Maybe he's meeting someone."

"I just hope he does something to incriminate himself." Suzie sighed as she watched Freddy's car turn into the parking lot of the truck stop. There were several semi-trucks lined up along one side of the parking lot. A small gas station, that appeared to be closed, stood in the middle of the pavement. "Who could he be meeting here?"

"Maybe we should drive past." Mary frowned. "He's going to notice if we turn in after him. There aren't any other cars around."

"But if we drive past, we won't have any idea what he's up to." Suzie's heart pounded as she realized that she needed to make a quick decision.

"If you pull in that entrance, the trucks should

block the view of our car." Mary pointed to a second entrance farther along the road.

"Perfect, Mary." Suzie smiled as she turned into the second entrance. She pulled up behind the row of trucks. "He parked over there." She pointed out the gold sedan. "But if he's meeting someone, I still don't see anyone else around."

As Suzie spoke, the door of the cab of the truck she'd parked behind, swung open. One man climbed down, then a second. Suzie's heart raced as she took in the sight of their suits and long coats. Were they the men Paul had seen?

"Who are they?" Mary whispered as she watched the two men walk towards the gold sedan. With her eyes focused on them, she never noticed the third man that stepped out of the cab, and then headed straight for their car.

The sharp knock of his knuckles on her window made her jump.

"Suzie!" Mary pushed down the lock on her door.

"Too late for that, I'm afraid." The man smiled. He was short, but quite muscular, and the way he smiled made Mary's stomach churn.

"Excuse us." Suzie started to turn the car back on.

The man stepped in front of the car, then pulled a gun from his waistband. As he pointed it at the windshield, he smiled again.

"Time to get out of the car, ladies."

"Mary, do what he says." Suzie shot her a look. "We need to be very careful, no one knows we're here."

"I'm not sure that I can get out." Mary shuddered as she reached for the door handle.

"Just take a deep breath. We'll get out together." Suzie looked into her eyes. "I'm going to get us out of this, I promise."

"What's going on here?" Freddy and the first two men walked towards the car as Suzie and Mary stepped out. "Put your gun away, Lorenzo!" He waved his hand at the short man.

The other two men stood on either side of Freddy. One was tall and thin, while the other was a bit shorter, and much wider.

"There's been some kind of mix-up." Suzie frowned as she looked straight at Freddy. "Just a little overreaction, I think."

"How did you even get here?" Freddy glared at her. "Did you follow me?"

"We just got a little lost." Suzie shrugged and laughed at the same time. "That's all. When I saw your car, well, I thought you must know where you're going, so I started following you. No harm intended." She held her hands up in the air. "Sorry to interrupt you, we'll be on our way."

"You were tailed by two old ladies?" The heavier man chuckled. "Some professional."

"Sorry Al. I didn't expect to be followed." Freddy shifted his attention to the two women, his eyes still narrowed.

"We didn't mean to follow you." Suzie smiled again as she grabbed Mary's hand. "So, our mistake really, we'll just be on our way." She steered Mary away from the group of men, back towards her car.

"Stop!" Al's commanding voice cracked through the air.

Suzie's grip tightened on Mary's hand as she froze.

Mary took a sharp breath and looked over at Suzie.

"Leaving so soon, ladies?" Al walked towards them. His cologne wafted through the air ahead of him as he stepped in front of them. "We haven't even been properly introduced." He held his hand out to Suzie. "I'm Al. And you are?"

"Not important." Suzie flashed him a smile.

"Just a scatter-brained, old lady, like you said. We can find our own way home, thanks."

"No, you can't." Al turned his hand over and placed it against her shoulder instead. "I'm sorry to tell you this, as I'm sure you're a perfectly nice person, but you have wandered into the wrong place, at the wrong time, and there will be consequences for that."

"That's really unnecessary." Suzie squirmed in an attempt to get out from under his grasp. In the same moment, cloth draped down over her head. It took her a second to realize it was a hood, and Lorenzo had likely been the one to put it on her. She reached up to pull it off, but her wrists were seized by someone behind her, she guessed it was Lorenzo.

Mary cried out as she witnessed Suzie's plight, but she didn't have time to react before the same thing happened to her.

"Please!" Mary tried to pull her hands free. "We didn't come here to cause any trouble."

"And yet you did." Al's cold voice made its way through the hoods. "But don't worry, I know exactly how to handle my problems."

"You're making a huge mistake. Just let us go, and you will be much better off." Suzie's voice wavered as she spoke. "We are very well known, and we will be missed very quickly."

"Well then, it's a good thing we're not sticking around town." Al chuckled. "Get them in the back of the truck, let's get moving."

Mary held her breath as she felt someone grab her by the arm. She fought the urge to pull away, or resist. She didn't want to give anyone an excuse to take care of Al's problem right then and there. As her stomach flipped, she wondered where exactly they were being taken. She heard Suzie's muffled breathing not far behind her.

"Get up there." The man beside her commanded as he gave her a light push against the tailgate of a vehicle.

A truck? Mary tried to see through the hood, but the material was too thick to even let much light in. Nervously, she tried to raise her leg.

"My knees," she whispered as pain shot through her knee. "I'm afraid they're not very good."

"Great." The man sighed. Then he hooked his arm around her waist.

Mary gasped as she was hoisted into the back of the truck. She knew it was no simple task for the man as she was not a skinny woman. Again, she thought about struggling, and again she talked herself out of it. Al's plan was to drive them some-where. That meant there would still be time for them to escape. But if she drew the wrath of any of her captors before that, there might not be any time left at all. Seconds later she heard the scuffle of Suzie climbing into the truck, along with a few words trying to convince whoever guided her inside to release her. Her words were punctuated by the sound of the truck doors slamming shut.

Mary tried to scoot closer to Suzie, but with her hands bound she found it very difficult to move much at all. Beyond the length of the truck, she heard its large engine roar to life. Wherever they were headed, Al had commanded them to get moving, and they were obeying that command. She squeezed her eyes shut tight and tried to think of anything positive about the situation. She was still alive. So was Suzie. That meant they still had a chance. She just had to stay focused on that.

CHAPTER 23

"*M*ary?" Suzie whispered. She felt the cloth against her lips and wondered how long she would have to wear the hood. "Where are we?"

"I'm not sure." Mary shifted her legs, then gasped as pain bolted through them. "I think we're still moving."

Suzie closed her eyes. She didn't need to. The hood made everything dark. But she still wanted to block out the situation she'd gotten them both into, even more. Why had she followed a man who was most certainly a murderer?

"I'm sorry, Mary. We shouldn't be here. If it wasn't for me—"

"Stop." Mary sighed. "It's not your fault, Suzie.

We both wanted to know what he was up to. Neither of us expected this to happen."

"Maybe, but all I had to do was drive the other way." Suzie stretched her wrists against the rope tied around them. "Maybe we can find a way out of this once the truck stops."

"Maybe." Mary rested her head back against the side of the truck. She could feel the vibrations carry through the metal surface. Yes, they were definitely still moving. But to where? She wanted them to keep driving forever, but she was also aware that every mile they drove away from Garber, was one more mile between them and anyone who might be able to help them.

Suzie's chest ached with fear as she tried to figure out exactly how they might escape. With their hands tied, and faces covered, they were at the mercy of their captors. "Suzie, we have to see if there's anything in this truck that can help us. We're going to need to surprise them if we have any hope of getting away. If we can find something to cut our hands free with, that would be a big help."

"Let's start with these hoods." Suzie grunted as she pushed her body towards the sound of Mary's voice. "If I can get my head to your hands, you can pull my hood off, then I can do the same for you." She felt her head strike Mary's hip. "Almost there."

"I can't reach." Mary stretched her hands as far as she could. "Can you get any closer?"

"I'm trying." Suzie wriggled across the floor.

"Got it." Mary tugged the hood free from Suzie's head.

"Oh, thank you." Suzie sighed, then pushed herself up into a sitting position. "Okay Mary, your turn. You're going to have to lay down for me to reach the hood. Just go slow and be careful."

Mary didn't have the chance to go slow or be careful. The truck suddenly jerked to the side, and she slid right across it and slammed into the wall.

"Ouch." She winced.

"Are you okay?" Suzie tried to get to her feet, but the truck rocked again, this time in the other direction. "Who is driving this thing?" She huffed.

Mary's eyes widened as she felt bumps and jerks ripple through the truck. Her stomach lurched as she realized that she wasn't just dizzy or off-balance, the whole truck was off-balance.

"Suzie, I think we're going down! I don't think anyone is driving!"

"Oh no!" Suzie cried out. "Find anything to hold on to, Mary, anything!"

Mary ran her hands along the wall behind her and found a strap that dangled from it. She clung to it tightly as the truck continued to lurch down what she guessed was the side of a mountain or hill.

"Do you think this is how Al meant to get rid of us?" Mary blinked back tears behind the hood that still covered her face.

"I don't think so." Suzie braced herself the best she could against the floor of the truck. "I don't think this was part of the plan."

The truck groaned, and then finally came to a stop. Suzie slid across the floor towards Mary. She could tell the truck had stopped at an angle. Which meant it could possibly begin to fall again.

"Suzie, are you okay?" Mary turned towards her.

"Let me get that off your head." Suzie tilted her body against the wall of the truck until she could reach the hood on Mary's head. "There." She smiled at the sight of her friend's face. "See, we're going to be just fine."

"I don't think I understand your definition of fine." Mary blinked at her. Then she noticed the hook on the end of the strap she held. "Maybe we can use this to get our hands free."

"Good plan." Suzie nodded. "Let's get back to

back. I can use the hook to cut through the rope on your hands."

"Do you think the others are still in the cab of the truck?" Mary positioned her back towards Suzie's.

"I'm not sure, but I don't want to wait to find out."

Suzie began to work the hook through the rope as fast as she could, however the point was not very sharp. Before she could make any progress, the door on the back of the truck began to rattle.

"Hello?" Freddy called out. "Hello, are you alive in there?"

Suzie froze.

Mary held her breath. She had no idea what the best way was to answer that question.

There wasn't time to decide whether to answer, as the door swung open before Suzie could speak a single word.

"Oh, thank goodness." Freddy stared at them. "Are either of you hurt?"

"No, I don't think so." Suzie stared back at him. "But you are." She watched a stream of blood trickle down his forehead.

"Yeah, I hit my head pretty good." Freddy wiped

the blood away. "Let's go, we need to get out of here. I think the truck is leaking fuel."

"We're not going anywhere with you." Mary shied back against the side of the truck.

"Look, I didn't sign up for this, okay?" Freddy sighed. "I got involved in this whole thing by accident. My cousin hooked me into it. He has a gambling debt with these guys and he had to help them to get it cleared. He told me it was time to expand the family business, that he knew of a place in Garber that we could easily smuggle product out. He said all I had to do was get a boat and bribe a few locals."

"So, what went wrong?" Suzie asked.

"I get here, and I figured out that I'm being watched by a private investigator. I never would have known it, but I was at Cheney's when he had an argument with an old client. I knew then, I'd been made." Freddy shook his head. "I think he thought it was his lucky day when I sat down next to him. I don't think he knew I knew who he was. I think he thought he might be able to get information out of me."

"You killed him?" Suzie looked into his eyes.

"I didn't mean to. I had no choice but to get rid of him for a while. I just wanted to make him sick so he would not be able to continue snooping and would go away. These guys my cousin got me mixed up with, they are killers. I knew they would come after me in a second if they thought I led the investigator to them. So, I took some powder from the supply I was smuggling, and I sprinkled it over his mashed potatoes. I honestly didn't know it would kill him. I didn't even know what it was. I just wanted to get my hands on his phone to see what evidence he had and to get him out of the way for a while." Freddy shook his head.

"But you killed him?" Mary grimaced.

"I didn't want to kill him. Once he was dead, I knew I was in a lot of trouble. I've just been trying to get rid of this product to clear my cousin's debt to them and get out of Garber, but Al and his guys kept dragging their feet." Freddy slammed his hand against the door of the truck. "Look, I may be a criminal, I may be someone who doesn't make the best choices, but I couldn't let those monsters kill you two. That's why I crashed the truck."

"What happened to the other guys?" Mary asked.

"They are in the truck. They are pretty messed up, but I don't know how long they will be out for. You've got to come with me, before they wake up."

"We'll be fine on our own, thanks." Suzie narrowed her eyes. She wasn't sure whether to believe his story, but she certainly wasn't going to trust him.

"Cut us free first." Mary turned her back to Freddy and held out her hands. "That way we know we can trust you."

"Fine." Freddy frowned and pulled a knife from his pocket. He sliced through the rope on Mary's wrists, then did the same for Suzie's. "There." He tucked the knife back into his pocket.

"Freddy!" Al's voice carried from the front of the truck. "Freddy, when I find you, you're a dead man!"

"We're too late!" Freddy gasped.

"On your knees!" A voice boomed from behind Freddy.

"Wes?" Mary caught sight of him with his gun pointed at Freddy and relief flooded through her.

Behind Wes, was what appeared to be an army of police officers, including Jason.

"Are you hurt?" Wes looked past Freddy at the two of them.

"No, we're okay." Suzie smiled and hugged Mary. "We're okay now."

It took some time for Suzie and Mary to make

their way back up the side of the mountain. As they walked, Wes lingered close beside them.

"Jason finally managed to contact Ginger's boss. Some chemicals at his lab went missing and he thought it was an inside job, so on Ginger's recommendation he hired Jerome to investigate it. Once he started investigating it, it apparently led him to Garber. The information you sent to Jason helped us work this out. He sent me the articles that you'd found because he knew the Mennossi crime family was tied to a few recent crimes in the area. Jason managed to link Freddy to his cousin whose photo matched a known associate of the Mennossi's. Jerome must have followed the same leads. The robbery at the lab led Jerome here. Freddy's cousin worked at the lab and he stole the stuff. Freddy was meant to help him smuggle it out. The trail led from Freddy to his cousin to the Mennossis. Then, Paul went in to see Jason because he thought Freddy might have been following you, Suzie. That's when we knew we had to find Freddy right away. Luckily, the camera at the dock had caught the license plate on Freddy's car. Garber and Parish PD worked together to find you as fast as we could. We tracked you to the truck stop, and then we were able to track the truck. I'm only sorry it took us so long to get to you."

"Well, I'm sorry that we were stuck in that truck in the first place." Suzie shook her head.

"It's not your fault, Suzie." Mary gave her a quick hug. "The important thing is that we are safe now."

"Yes, that is the most important thing." Wes wrapped his arm around Mary's waist and helped her up onto the road. He turned back to reach for Suzie's hand, but before he could, Paul's hand reached out from a few steps beside him.

"Suzie." He pulled her close to him. "I'm so sorry that I didn't realize what was happening sooner."

"Are you kidding, Paul? If it wasn't for you, we never would have been found." Suzie rested her head against his chest. "I'm just glad all of this is over." She hugged him as tight as she could.

"I wish I could get my hands on Freddy." Paul growled as he watched Jason escort Freddy to a patrol car. Other officers escorted Al and his associates as well.

"Don't be too hard on him." Suzie turned to look at Freddy as he was placed in the car. "In the end, I think he really didn't want to hurt us. He helped save us. From what he said I don't even think he meant to kill Jerome. At least now we know what happened."

"Let me take you home." Paul kissed her cheek. "I saved you a cinnamon roll."

"Oh sweetheart." Suzie smiled as she looked into his eyes. "You really do love me."

"I do." Paul laughed and pulled her close for a kiss.

The End

ALSO BY CINDY BELL

DUNE HOUSE COZY MYSTERIES

Seaside Secrets

Boats and Bad Guys

Treasured History

Hidden Hideaways

Dodgy Dealings

Suspects and Surprises

Ruffled Feathers

A Fishy Discovery

Danger in the Depths

Celebrities and Chaos

Pups, Pilots and Peril

Tides, Trails and Trouble

Racing and Robberies

Athletes and Alibis

Manuscripts and Deadly Motives

CHOCOLATE CENTERED COZY MYSTERIES

The Sweet Smell of Murder

A Deadly Delicious Delivery

A Bitter Sweet Murder

A Treacherous Tasty Trail

Pastry and Peril

Trouble and Treats

Fudge Films and Felonies

Custom-Made Murder

Skydiving, Soufflés and Sabotage

Christmas Chocolates and Crimes

Hot Chocolate and Homicide

Chocolate Caramels and Conmen

Picnics, Pies and Lies

Devils Food Cake and Drama

DONUT TRUCK COZY MYSTERIES

Deadly Deals and Donuts

Fatal Festive Donuts

Bunny Donuts and a Body

Strawberry Donuts and Scandal

SAGE GARDENS COZY MYSTERIES

Birthdays Can Be Deadly

Money Can Be Deadly

Trust Can Be Deadly

Ties Can Be Deadly

Rocks Can Be Deadly

Jewelry Can Be Deadly

Numbers Can Be Deadly

Memories Can Be Deadly

Paintings Can Be Deadly

Snow Can Be Deadly

Tea Can Be Deadly

Greed Can Be Deadly

Clutter Can Be Deadly

WAGGING TAIL COZY MYSTERIES

Murder at Pawprint Creek

Murder at Pooch Park

Murder at the Pet Boutique

A Merry Murder at St. Bernard Cabins

Murder at the Dog Training Academy

BEKKI THE BEAUTICIAN COZY MYSTERIES

Hairspray and Homicide

A Dyed Blonde and a Dead Body

Mascara and Murder

Pageant and Poison

Conditioner and a Corpse

Mistletoe, Makeup and Murder

Hairpin, Hair Dryer and Homicide

Blush, a Bride and a Body

Shampoo and a Stiff

Cosmetics, a Cruise and a Killer

Lipstick, a Long Iron and Lifeless

Camping, Concealer and Criminals

Treated and Dyed

A Wrinkle-Free Murder

A MACARON PATISSERIE COZY MYSTERY SERIES

Sifting for Suspects

Recipes and Revenge

Mansions, Macarons and Murder

NUTS ABOUT NUTS COZY MYSTERIES

A Tough Case to Crack

A Seed of Doubt

Roasted Penuts and Peril

HEAVENLY HIGHLAND INN COZY MYSTERIES

Murdering the Roses

Dead in the Daisies

Killing the Carnations

Drowning the Daffodils

Suffocating the Sunflowers

Books, Bullets and Blooms

A Deadly Serious Gardening Contest

A Bridal Bouquet and a Body

Digging for Dirt

WENDY THE WEDDING PLANNER COZY MYSTERIES

Matrimony, Money and Murder

Chefs, Ceremonies and Crimes

Knives and Nuptials

Mice, Marriage and Murder

ABOUT THE AUTHOR

Cindy Bell is a USA Today and Wall Street Journal Bestselling Author. She is the author of the cozy mystery series Wagging Tail, Donut Truck, Dune House, Sage Gardens, Chocolate Centered, Macaron Patisserie, Nuts about Nuts, Bekki the Beautician, Heavenly Highland Inn and Wendy the Wedding Planner.

Cindy has always loved reading, but it is only recently that she has discovered her passion for writing romantic cozy mysteries. She loves walking along the beach thinking of the next adventure her characters can embark on.

You can sign up for her newsletter so you are notified of her latest releases at http://www.cindybellbooks.com.

Made in the USA
Las Vegas, NV
20 May 2023

72318404R00134